SO GOOD

_____

JENIKA SNOW

SO GOOD

By Jenika Snow

www.JenikaSnow.com

Jenika_Snow@Yahoo.com

Copyright © May 2019 by Jenika Snow

Photographer: Wander Aguiar

Cover Model: Jonny James & Amanda Joan

Image provided by: Wander book club

Cover design by: Designs by Dana

Editor: Kasi Alexander

Content Editor/Proofreader: All Encompassing books

Matthew

Ivy. So sweet and young, so innocent and mine, even though I was crossing a line by simply desiring her.

My step-brother's daughter. Forbidden, taboo. I should stay away, but in my mind I'd already claimed her, already made the decision I couldn't let her go.

If wanting her was wrong ... I didn't want to be right.

Ivy

I was still in high school, hadn't even experienced the world, but I already knew who I wanted to spend my life with.

Matthew.

He was someone I could never be with, yet here I was, feeling him, touching him ... being with him. It was all so perfect until it wasn't, until my father found out ... until my world was turned upside down.

And through it all Matthew was there, telling me he wouldn't give me up, wouldn't let me go.

But could he keep that promise during the fallout?

1

***

Ivy

My very first memories involved Matthew, the way he'd held my hand as he took me to the park. The way he'd helped me on the swing and then pushed me. He'd watched me when my mother and father had been at work, playing board games with me, sneaking hot fudge sundaes before dinner.

He'd been a constant presence in my life always. I trusted him more than anyone else, knew that he'd never let anyone hurt me.

I remember looking up at him, the sun behind him, the glare intense, and thinking he was a superhero.

My superhero.

And when a little boy had been picking on me, Matthew had been there to tell him that treating girls with respect and kindness was the only way to grow up being a good man.

He was Matthew, *my* Matthew, my best friend, my father's step-brother.

My step-uncle.

He was family, the one person that I knew would never let me down. And after my mother died in a wrong place, wrong time kind of thing, I never thought the world would be right again. I was young, so young that as time went on, I started to feel like I would be okay, that things would get better.

So I'd focused on school, knowing that she'd want me to focus on what made me happy.

And I don't know when it had changed, when my feelings for Matthew had started changing from adoration and admiration to ... desire.

It was wrong, a sin, right? He was family, and although not a blood relative, I'd only ever known him as Uncle Matthew.

I was eighteen and finishing up my senior year of high school. I had plans, ambitions.

I had a future.

And I should have been happy, excited about it all, but over the summer something had changed within me. Something had grown, like a branch of a tree that was twisted and barren, reaching for the sun because that's all it knew.

And Matthew was my sun.

He was all I knew.

I'd felt something shift and turn in me, clawing to get out.

Matthew was outside in the garden, his short dark hair slightly damp at his temples from perspiration. He was installing a new walkway, not something we especially needed, but Matthew liked to stay busy. He liked to work with his hands.

The way his biceps flexed as he worked on the cobblestone had my heart racing. The sight of his tattoo-covered flesh had my body reacting in ways I'd only ever felt with him.

His white T-shirt had smudges of dirt on it, wet from sweat, the sun beating down on him.

My sun.

I was drawn to him like a moth to a flame, my ultimate death awaiting.

He lifted his arm and wiped the sweat from his forehead, his bicep flexing. He was muscular. Having worked in construction most of his adult life had made his body powerful, like a tank.

My hands started aching and I looked down to see

my fingers twisted together in my shirt almost violently. I loosened my hold, breathing out slowly, and lifted my head to look back out the window, only to see Matthew looking at me. The air left me viciously and I should have glanced away, but I found myself transfixed at the sight of him, at how he drew out this reaction from me.

Time had no meaning in that moment, no physical hold on me.

I felt a tightness claim me instantly when I saw Mara, our very attractive, very available next-door neighbor walk up to Matthew with a bottle of water in her hand and a come-fuck-me smile plastered on her face.

"Earth to Ivy."

I blinked a few times and pulled my focus away from the window. My cheeks felt hot, the very real possibility that Georgia had seen me watching Matthew embarrassing me.

"I'm here." I cleared my throat and walked back to the table, sitting down across from her. We were in the last month of high school, our senior year, and I couldn't focus.

I hadn't been able to for months now, ever since I realized what I'd been feeling for Matthew was most definitely not appropriate.

I brought my pencil up to my mouth and started chewing on the end as I zoned out. I could hear Georgia talking, but I wasn't focused on what she said.

I didn't know how long I sat there, but I soon heard the side door open and my heart jumped into my throat. I knew it was Matthew coming inside.

Acting like I had my shit together in that moment was easier said than done, especially seeing as I felt flushed and aroused.

I straightened and looked out toward the hallway, watching as Matthew came into view. He pulled a rag out of his pocket and started wiping the sweat from his forehead, then dragged it down and over the back of his neck.

My fingers were wrapped tightly around the pencil, so hard that it was almost a little painful. He glanced over at us and grinned, giving me a wink and making butterflies move wildly in my stomach, sucking the very air from my lungs.

He stepped into the entryway and leaned against the doorframe, crossing his big, muscular arms over his chest. "You girls studying hard?"

He glanced between Georgia and me and I cleared my throat, hoping he couldn't see how affected I was by his presence.

"Hardly studying is more like it." Georgia giggled

and I glanced over at her, seeing this dreamy-eyed expression on her face.

But I couldn't blame her for being attracted to Matthew. He was all man and I'd fallen down that rabbit hole, too.

He gave me one last look, the corner of his mouth kicking up in a smirk, before the sound of my dad calling for him rang out.

"See ya later, girls," he said and walked away. I couldn't help but sigh at the way his powerful body moved so stealthily.

"Good God. Your uncle is hot as hell," Georgia said.

I glanced over at her and saw her fanning her face, her cheeks pink. Her gaze was locked on mine and she grinned before shrugging.

"He's too old for us, Georgia," I muttered and then realized what I'd said. I glanced up, feeling my eyes widen, but thankfully she hadn't heard the slip in my comment. I should have said he was too old for *her*. I most definitely shouldn't have said he was too old for *us*.

"What can I say? He's every girl's fantasy."

I shook my head and glanced away, hoping she didn't see how much this conversation affected me. I didn't want my secret to come out, definitely not like this.

Lusting after my uncle? Related or not, he'd been

in my life for, well, ever. And no doubt people would see my feelings as wrong and sick, taboo.

Maybe I shouldn't care what people thought. But the very idea of Matthew thinking those things was painful. So keeping this to myself, taking it to my grave, was for the best.

2

Ivy

"Party at your house this weekend? Count me the hell in," Georgia said after she guzzled half her water bottle.

"Calling it a party might be exaggerating. It'll just be my dad, Matthew, and you. I'm not really feeling anything big."

"Ivy, it's your nineteenth birthday, your last year of high school. What do you mean not feeling anything big?"

I shrugged. "I don't know. It's just not a big deal."

Georgia looked shocked. "Well, it's your birthday so your decision." She smiled. "But I think a party would be cool." She shrugged and went back to eating her food. And then she started talking about Marcus, one of the guys in her class who'd been showing interest in me the whole school year.

That was the thing about Georgia; she didn't linger on certain subjects, and I was thankful for that. I didn't want to talk about a party, because the truth was as much as I would've liked having friends over to celebrate my nineteenth birthday, there was something going on with my dad.

I'd seen the change in him over the last week or so, how distant he'd been, the lack of conversation, his overall contact with me. He didn't even act happy, and I'd felt that change thicken the air.

He seemed stressed, and the last thing I wanted to do was bring up something so mundane as a birthday party when he was obviously dealing with stuff.

"So, what about Marcus?" Georgia said, breaking through my thoughts.

I wrinkled my nose and shook my head.

"Seriously?" Georgia asked. "He's one of the hottest guys in school. Not to mention he's like totally into you."

"He's not my type," I said, really not wanting to talk about Marcus or any other guy, for that matter.

I wasn't interested in him. I wasn't interested in anyone but Matthew. Then again, look at how that was going for me. It's not like I could actually be with him. Not like I could actually admit to him how I felt, or anyone else for that matter. And this wasn't just infatuation. This wasn't just some schoolgirl crush. I loved him.

I was in love with him in a way I probably shouldn't be, in a way that would seem disgusting to society, would seem immoral and just ... wrong.

It was taboo to be in love with a family member, even if said family member wasn't related by anything but marriage.

But I didn't care. I knew what I wanted, who I cared about, and that was all that mattered to me.

———

I PULLED into the driveway of my house, my thoughts on what Georgia had said. Maybe I should just try and push away my feelings for Matthew and go after someone my own age ... someone who wasn't connected to me in a forbidden manner. But even thinking about being with someone else left a bad taste in my mouth. It had my stomach clenching and all kinds of wrong thoughts filling me.

I cut the engine, my heart doing a little flip when I realized Matthew's truck was parked in the driveway. My dad's car was right beside his, which seemed a bit odd seeing as how at this hour he should have been at work.

After grabbing my bag and the few textbooks I'd thrown on the passenger seat, I headed up to the front door.

As soon as I stepped inside, I felt something was off. It was this thickness in the air, this electricity that moved over my arms. I felt my chest tighten as I set my backpack on the floor by the wall and stepped farther inside.

I looked in the living room but didn't see my father, so I headed down the short hallway and went into the kitchen. I saw my dad and Matthew sitting at the table, my father's head lowered as if he were upset or disappointed about something. He had his hands clasped in front of him on top of the old, scarred dining room table.

I glanced at Matthew, who was leaning back in his chair, his big body tense, something I could tell even from a distance. He glanced up at me and I felt my chest tighten even further at the look he gave me.

Something was wrong.

"What's going on?" My father looked up then, this surprised expression on his face. He hadn't known I'd come home, maybe didn't want me to see him like this. "Guys, what's going on?" I asked when they didn't say anything and just stared at me.

"Ivy, come sit down."

My movements were slow as I walked to the table.

Matthew reached out and pulled the chair out for me and I sat down, glancing between the two of them.

"I'm just gonna cut right to it because I've already been keeping it from you for the past week."

My heart jumped into my throat and I swallowed, my hands starting to shake. Every bad thought filled my head. Was he sick? Hurt?

I placed my hands on my lap, curling them together so my fingers were intertwined.

"Okay," I said softly and tried to act like I wasn't nervous as hell. My father took a deep breath and leaned back in the chair, staring me in the eyes.

"I lost my job last week."

For a moment, I couldn't process his words. I didn't even know what they meant. Then, slowly reality set in. "Okay," I said again and looked between him and Matthew. "What exactly does that mean? We're okay financially, right?"

I wasn't an idiot. I knew that him losing his job wasn't good, but maybe he'd found a new one already?

"It just means things are going to be hard, but it'll work out." Matthew was the one to respond and I glanced at him. He seemed so sure, so calm.

I glanced back at my dad. "How did you lose your job? You've been there for as long as I can remember." I instantly saw this discomfort surround him. He was nervous, looking away from me, not able to hold my gaze with his.

And then he looked up at Matthew, and I could see that my uncle knew what was going on, knew why my father had lost his job.

And I knew it was bad.

"Dad?" I looked back at my father. We'd always been truthful with each other, but I could see right now him being honest with me was hard.

He cleared his throat and shifted on the chair several times before finally exhaling. "I started a relationship with a coworker." He paused for a moment and I knew he wasn't finished. "It's frowned upon to fraternize in the work area."

Confusion filled me even more. "Surely something like that, they'd give you a warning instead of firing you? Losing your job seems extreme." I didn't understand any of this and could see on my dad's face he was worried.

"It wasn't just that we had a relationship and worked together, but I was seeing my employer's daughter." He cleared his throat and shifted on the seat over and over again, his nervousness tangible. "His twenty-year-old daughter."

I saw the frantic look on his face, and knew that him telling me he was sleeping with a woman so young had him panicked because she was so close to my age.

But in that moment, I looked over at Matthew, my love for him growing. I was soon to be nineteen. He was in his thirties. The age gap between us was immense. But I didn't care.

I looked over at my father again. I wasn't going to touch on this subject, wasn't going to ask questions or delve deeper. "So what now?" was all I said. It was all that I could utter.

"Now we figure things out." Matthew was the one to speak. "My lease is up and I'm going to move in to help your dad out."

Matthew was moving in?

"It'll help take some stress off your dad so he can find a job and not worry so much about bills and watching over you."

I wanted to tell him that I was nearly an adult, that I didn't need looking after, but the truth was the very thought of Matthew here constantly was almost like a dream come true.

I glanced over at my father and saw he looked dejected. "Did you love her?" The only woman I'd ever seen my father with had been my mother. So this was all a little bit strange, definitely new.

His throat worked as he swallowed, and I could practically feel the tension in the air.

"I care about her," he said and I heard the genuine tone in his voice. "And so I refused to stop seeing her—"

"Which had you losing your job," I finished for him. He nodded. My throat felt so tight it hurt. "Are we going to lose the house? Will we have to move?"

"No," my father said adamantly.

"We're going to make sure you stay exactly where you are, that this house remains yours," Matthew said.

I glanced over at him, feeling dazed, confused, and in a fog. How could I be upset at my dad for standing by his convictions, for being with someone he cared for when I was staring at the man I loved ... the man I had no business being with?

3

Ivy

My mind was in a haze as I stared out at the backyard, the sun starting to set, the colors of orange, red, and pink splashing across the dusky sky.

My mind was a whirl at everything that had transpired this past week. Matthew moving his things in, taking the spare bedroom beside mine. My father on the phone constantly looking for temporary work until he could find something permanent. And all the while I wondered how things would really play out.

It made me feel a little braver, that perhaps I could tell Matthew how I felt. If my father cared about somebody so young, surely he would understand my feelings for Matthew?

I heard the backdoor open and glanced over my shoulder to see Matthew stepping out and onto the porch. It was as if my thoughts had conjured him and I felt my heartrate instantly pick up. I shifted on the plastic lounge chair, bringing my legs closer to my chest so now my feet were braced on the edge, my toes dangling slightly off.

"Hey," he said in his deep, masculine voice. He moved closer to me and took a seat in the chair beside mine.

"Hi," I said softly and continued to stare straight ahead.

For long moments we didn't speak, and the silence was deafening. I could feel the tension in the air, the stress. But maybe that was just from me. Maybe how I felt was being projected.

And I hated that possibility.

I hated it had gotten to this point, where I didn't know what was up from down.

"What's on your mind?" Matthew asked, and I looked at him.

He was already watching me, the shadows playing around his big body, the tattoos visible underneath the thin white Henley he wore. His hair was a little bit disheveled, as if he'd been running his fingers through it.

I wondered how stressful this was for him. He

seemed so calm and collected all the time, especially in the face of tension. But how did he really feel?

"I'm just thinking about how I don't know what's going on or what the future holds." I was honest, wanting to ask him so many things, but also afraid to delve deeper. I didn't want him to be standoffish with me, didn't want that weird vibe bouncing between us. "I'm wondering what my father's going to do about work. I'm wondering what he's going to do about this new relationship he's in." I swallowed the thick lump in my throat and looked at the back yard once more, staring at the sun as it started to set behind the horizon. The silence was our companion for long moments, but I felt Matthew's gaze on me. I looked back at him. "What are you thinking about?"

He lifted his hand and rubbed the back of his neck, the expression on his face telling me he was thinking about my question. "I'm thinking about you." More silence. "I'm thinking about how this is all affecting you." He cleared his throat.

I wanted him to look at me again, wanted to feel his gaze on me as if it were his finger stroking along my body.

"I'm thinking how I want to protect you from all of this, and how I wish you weren't feeling this lost and helpless." He looked at me again and when his eyes met mine it was like the spark of electricity traveled right through the center of my body. "But I'm here now and I'm not going anywhere. I'll make sure everything works out. I promise, Ivy." He reached out and took my hand and gave it a light squeeze.

My heart started racing at that small, innocent touch. His hand was so much bigger than mine, his palms and fingers callused from the hard manual work he did day in and day out. His skin was warm, golden brown as if it were kissed from the sun.

I wanted to hold on to that, take it in, let it consume me.

I opened my mouth, the words right there on the tip of my tongue.

I love you. I love you. I'm so in love with you.

Those words repeated over and over in my head like this mantra, so close to being free, my deepest, darkest secret ready to be spilled. But the sound of his phone vibrating in his pocket had me swallowing them, had them hiding deep down inside of me once more.

For a moment, it looked like he didn't want to break the connection, this moment between us, but when he fished it out of his pocket and looked at the screen, I saw the seriousness on his face.

"It's work. I have to take it." He gave my hand a squeeze and I felt my belly tighten in response.

He stood, and I watched him walk away and go back into the house.

All I wanted to do was call him back, to be honest and tell him that I loved him, that it might be wrong, that he was my uncle, but that there was nobody else in the world I'd ever give my heart to but him.

———

Matthew

I ended the call and shoved my cell back in my pocket, my heart racing and my hands sweaty. My reaction had nothing to do with the work call I'd just taken, and everything to do with being out there on the porch with Ivy.

My Ivy.

What I felt for her was twisted, taboo. She was my niece, for fuck's sake. And although we weren't blood related, I was her family, had watched her grow into the beautiful woman she was today.

What was wrong with me? She was so innocent and vulnerable, so impressionable. And the way she looked at me told me my feelings weren't one-sided.

She looked at me with adoration and love, as if I could give her the world if she asked.

And I would, in a heartbeat.

But she was so young, only eighteen. I was old enough to be her father.

I was her step-uncle.

So wrong, yet I couldn't help myself with her, couldn't control my feelings.

I walked over to the window and could see her standing by the banister now, leaning against it. She was gorgeous, but the things I felt for her were wrong. I felt as if I were breaking the law, going against a moral code.

Betraying my brother.

I heard him start to come down the stairs and looked away from Ivy, watching as he stepped onto the landing.

He glanced up, and seemed surprised that I was standing there.

"Hey," he said and scratched his jaw, the sound of his nails going over his scruff loud in the foyer.

I cleared my throat, feeling guilty as hell for just thinking about Ivy in the way I was. "How are you holding up?" Over the last week we hadn't spoken too much about what was going down, not anything in depth.

He loved his former employer's daughter, refused to stop seeing her, so he'd lost his job because he broke the rules.

Stephan looked exhausted, as if he'd been put

through the wringer.

"Honestly? I feel like I'm hanging on by a thread."

I felt like shit, because here was my brother going through all this crap in his life, and I was thinking about wanting Ivy in some pretty obscene ways. My desires and needs were so minimal compared to the priorities at hand.

I nodded, not knowing what to say, how to make things better.

"But ain't shit to be done but move forward." He exhaled. "I want to thank you for moving in and helping me. I know I've only been out of work for a week, but I'm already starting to feel the pressure of not finding a job, having to explain to potential employers why I lost my previous one, and then the bills are mounting. It's all pretty fucking stressful."

I walked up to him and clapped him on the back. "We're family. I'd do anything for you and Ivy." And on the heels of that I thought about my love for her, how for the past year I'd wanted her like no other.

It was as if something in me had been awoken when she turned eighteen. But I kept those feelings hidden like my life depended on it. And I suppose it did.

I didn't want to cross that line. I didn't want to betray the people I trusted, who trusted me, and who I loved. But I saw Ivy as a woman. I saw her as *mine*.

4

Ivy

The lights were dimmed by Matthew and a moment later my father came out holding a small cake with three candles in the center of it. The glow illuminated his face, a genuine smile spread across his mouth.

He set the cake in front of me and I smiled, knowing that the past few weeks had been really hard on him, and still were. Despite him searching for a job, he hadn't found anything and I knew it was wearing him down.

I didn't know if it was because of the reason he'd lost his job and therefore future employers were staying away, but either way it broke my heart seeing him like this, knowing he was struggling.

And then there was the matter of him being involved with the woman in question, and how juggling everything had to be hard. I heard them talking on the phone on several occasions. But I guess I was too afraid to ask him about it, to want to meet her.

I suppose I found it a little weird knowing my father was involved with someone so young. And on the heels of that, though, I found it funny, hypocritical, or maybe even ironic, given my own situation.

Here I was, nineteen and in love with my step-uncle. I should have no issues with my father being with whomever he wanted, but I guess it was a little different seeing as he was my dad.

"Make a wish, honey," he said softly and sat down beside me, the grin still in place.

I looked over at Georgia, who sat on my other side. Then I glanced at Matthew, who stood over by the light switch, leaning against the wall with his arms crossed, his shirt pulled snug against his muscles.

What a sad excuse for a nineteenth birthday, I could practically hear Georgia say. And maybe she was right. But to me this was perfect. I was a low-key type of person, and the three people in this room were the ones I cared about the most.

Georgia was like family, like my sister. She'd been in this house more times than I could count, knew we really didn't have any family, and that I wasn't really close with anyone.

I looked down at the cake, at those three candles and the flames that danced as a light breeze picked up. I closed my eyes for a moment and then inhaled a second before I exhaled, extinguishing them. The scent of smoke instantly filled my nose.

When I opened my eyes, it was at the same time Matthew turned the lights on. Our gazes clashed, held. As my father started cutting the cake, and Georgia started talking to him about her plans for college this fall, all I could do was stare at Matthew.

My lips tingled from the idea of him kissing me, my heart raced from the thought of feeling him touch me, press up against me. But I knew nothing could happen. I knew nothing ever would.

This was my life, my broken love story.

How would I ever go on and find a man, marry him, have children with him, when my one true love was just feet from me, untouchable, unattainable ... forbidden?

"What did you wish for?" Georgia asked and I glanced over at her.

That I could be with Matthew and it would all work out. That I could love him without judgment.

I didn't tell her that, of course.

"I wished for world peace," I said, lying easily. She

snorted. I glanced over at Matthew, saw the way he swallowed, his throat working. Could he see the desire on my face whenever I looked at him? Could he see my love for him?

He kept me at arm's length and I hated it. I felt so lost, lonely. But the truth was, I wouldn't have changed my feelings for anything. I wouldn't have stopped them even if I'd known this would be the outcome.

For the next half hour we sat around the table and ate cake, my father telling stories of when I was younger, memories he had of my mother and me when I was a child. It had been so long since we'd talked about her, as if my father didn't want to bring up painful memories.

Death had a funny way of making you appreciate life, each day. It made you appreciate love even more.

Matthew sat at the end of the table, across from me, looking at me, barely speaking during that entire time. It was like he was another man, not the easygoing person I'd grown up with, that I looked up to.

And I hated that. I wanted things to be okay, no matter what was driving a wedge between us.

I wanted things okay for everyone.

———

"I WISH I COULD STAY," Georgia said.

"I know, and I wish you could too. But go help your sister with her school project. I'm just glad you were here. It would've even been an even sadder birthday if you hadn't been able to show up."

She chuckled and rolled her eyes. "It was fine and not pitiful at all. It was fun and your dad is hilarious." She got a serious expression on her face then. "How are you doing now?"

I shifted on my feet and shoved my hands in the pockets of my jeans. I shrugged. "I'm fine," I said, lying. "I mean, what else can I do, how can I really feel? It is what it is, right?"

"I mean, I guess. But it still sucks with the whole job thing."

I nodded, knowing that was the truth.

"And you haven't talked to your dad about his girlfriend yet? You haven't met her?"

I shook my head. "Truth is, I'm not even upset or feel weird about him dating someone so young." Because I harbored my own taboo feelings toward my uncle. "But even so, I don't know if I want to?" I phrased it like a question because the truth was I didn't know if I was ready to meet her.

Would it be weird given the fact I had feelings for Matthew, a much older man? Would it be too much like my father's relationship with a young girl? It was just so confusing.

There was a moment of silence and then I saw her expression change. I knew she was switching the topic and I silently thanked God for that.

She glanced over my shoulder, looking nervous all of a sudden. I turned and stared behind me to see what she was looking at, but there was nothing. When I faced her again, I felt my brows bunch in confusion. "What are you doing? Who are you looking for?"

She gave me this mischievous grin and then walked over to her bag, which she'd set on the floor by the front door when she'd first gotten here. I watched as she rifled around in it, and then a second later she pulled out a bottle of peach schnapps.

I felt my eyes widen as I saw the bottle, then quickly looked behind me, expecting my father or Matthew to be standing there about to give us the third degree for having liquor.

"Oh my God, Georgia. Where did you get that from?"

She grinned and tried to discreetly hand it to me, but the bottle was pretty big. I kept looking around, expecting Matthew or my father to walk in and see the exchange, as if we were shady people making a drug deal in an alley.

"Marcus has a friend who is twenty-one. Told him to buy me this so I could give it to you." She was still grinning like she had just given me the key to all the secrets of the world. "After the last couple of weeks you've had, I figured you might need something strong."

I looked down at it and then back up at her. "What am I supposed to do with it?"

She snorted and rolled her eyes. "Ivy, you drink it." Georgia started chuckling as if she'd had to really break it down for me and thought it was funny.

"Obviously, Georgia. But I don't drink."

Just as she was about to speak, her cell vibrated and she pulled it out of her coat pocket.

She looked at the screen and sighed. "It's my mom. I have to go. She's bitching at me because I'm not home yet."

She gave me a hug, the liquor bottle wedged between us, digging into my ribs. When she pulled back she look down at it and grinned again.

"And keep your schedule open for that party." She winked. "Have a good time." She wagged her brows at me as she glanced down at the alcohol. Then she turned, grabbed her bag off the floor, and headed out the door.

I stood there with this big bottle of liquor in my hands, telling myself I wasn't going to go to my room and drink alone. But then I heard my father's phone ringing. The way he answered it, his tone changing, becoming softer, sweeter, I knew he was talking to the woman he was seeing.

So I turned and headed upstairs, shut myself in my room, and unscrewed the top of the bottle.

The first swallow burned, but the longer I did it, the more I drank, the more it started to taste pretty damn good.

This might be a very bad idea. Or maybe it was the best one I'd had in a long time.

5

Ivy

I didn't know how long I stayed up in my room. An hour? Two?

It all blurred together.

I'd drunk a decent amount of the schnapps and was feeling a nice buzz. My body felt warm, my muscles kind of achy.

I found myself stumbling down the stairs, trying to be quiet because I knew my father had gone to bed. The last thing I needed was for him to see me this way and grill me on specifics.

I first went into the kitchen, got a glass of water, and drank that before refilling it. I wasn't trashed, but I had a pretty intense buzz going on.

I set the cup in the sink and it tipped over, the

sound seeming so loud. I thought for sure I'd woken him up. I froze, looking up at the ceiling, trying to tell if he was getting up. I had no idea if he could hear it. But maybe I should've been more concerned about Matthew catching me in this condition. He was, after all, far more intense than my dad.

But he'd left the house hours ago, right after Georgia had gone home. I'd heard him leave, the sound of his truck starting and driving off in the distance.

I closed my eyes and exhaled. Maybe some fresh air would do me some good. Maybe I just needed to go sit on the deck and let myself sober up.

I started walking out of the kitchen, feeling a little dizzy, and braced my hand on the wall to steady myself. Then I found my way toward the back door, gripped it, pulled it open, and a gust of fresh air moved over me. For a moment I just stood there, closing my eyes and letting that coolness move over me. It felt good, calming.

And for just a second I didn't feel buzzed at all. But then the sound of a floorboard creaking to my right had me snapping my eyes open and looking to the side. There, leaning against the banister with a bottle of whiskey in his hand, was Matthew.

He stared right at me, the shadows concealing his face, his big body seeming to dwarf the deck. I contemplated just leaving, heading back inside, maybe going to my room and sleeping this off. Because he'd know I had been drinking. I knew it.

But a part of me didn't want to leave. I found myself moving forward and stepping onto the deck. I shut the door behind me and tried to act sober.

It felt strange being here, seeing him when I was in this condition, when I knew how I felt about him. It felt different in the way that had me more tuned in to my love for him, as if my feelings were more heightened.

And I didn't know if I liked that, or if it scared the hell out of me.

But it looked like I wasn't smart enough to know better and turn away. It looked like they called alcohol *liquid courage* for a reason.

———

Matthew

As soon as I saw the back door open, I knew it was Ivy. I instantly smelled the sweet, floral fragrance that always seemed to surround her.

After everyone had eaten cake and talked, and after I'd overheard Ivy and Georgia talking, I went to the convenience store and bought a bottle of whiskey. It had been a combination of my feelings for her, the guilt I felt, but also this possessive and jealous side of me knowing she'd be going to a party.

I'd been her age once. I knew the shit that went down at those things.

And when I'd come back to the house with the purchase, I'd gone straight to the deck. I'd kept the porch light off and drank in the darkness.

For the last hour, I'd been nursing the fuck out of the bottle.

My feelings for her were growing stronger by the day, and I was afraid of being around her, afraid that I wouldn't be able to control myself, that my desires would overcome rationalization.

She stepped out onto the deck and closed the door behind her. I brought the bottle up to my mouth and took a drink, watching her the whole time. I'd been nursing this fucker and I still had half a bottle.

Drinking wasn't the way to solve my problems, but it sure was helping numb the pain I felt with the knowledge I could never have her.

I watched her as she came closer and braced herself against the banister, her hand curling around the edge of it. She seemed a little unsteady on her feet, and as the wind picked up, I could smell the scent of peaches and alcohol clinging to her.

"Hey," she said, and I heard the slight slurring of

her voice.

I knitted my brows, but didn't move closer. I didn't trust myself to. "Are you okay?" I set the bottle down on the ground beside me and straightened. I didn't want her seeing me drinking. Although I had a decent buzz going on, so not a whole lot fucking mattered right now.

But where Ivy was concerned, she was always my priority. She always mattered.

"I'm fine," she said.

But I knew that she'd been drinking. It was the way her eyes looked glossy, the fact that her pupils were dilated. Her cheeks were pink and her gait was unsteady. Not to mention she smelled of alcohol.

But Stephan didn't keep alcohol in the house, and I knew from inadvertently eavesdropping that she'd gotten it from Georgia.

"Georgia gave you liquor?" She didn't seem surprised I knew, and instead nodded. "What did you get drunk off of?" The protective side of me rose up instantly. I wanted to keep her safe, shelter her. I didn't want her to experience the nasty aftereffects of what drinking did to people. But then again, I was being a hypocrite because here I was with a half-empty bottle of whiskey on the ground beside me.

"Peach schnapps," she said instantly, not lying to me. That pleased me. But I was aggravated that she had been drinking, not because she was underage, not because she'd done it right under our noses. I was frustrated because I wanted to protect her even if that was from herself.

I didn't say anything because it wasn't my place to scold her, to tell her the dangers of drinking, how it brought your inhibitions down and made you vulnerable.

I didn't want to tell her any of that because my inhibitions were down right now, and the only thing I wanted to say was that I loved her. The only thing I wanted to do was bring her close to me and show her with my body how much I cared for her.

Instead, I stood there and stared at her, the porch light off, the glow from the moon making this silvery light wash across her. I should have kept my fucking mouth shut. I should have just gone inside, locked myself in my room, and jerked off to the thought of her, because that's all I'd ever be able to do where Ivy was concerned.

But instead I found my possessiveness and jealousy rising up as I thought about her around drunken assholes.

"I overheard Georgia remind you about a party." I reached down and picked up the bottle of whiskey, taking a drink from it as I watched her over the rim. "I don't have to remind you how unsafe those are, how there are little fuckers that will try and get in your pants because they'll see you're drinking and that your inhibitions are down."

She didn't respond right away, but I could assume she was confused by my sudden interrogation. I'd always kept my distance when it came to her personal life, and it had been easy as hell ... until she'd turned eighteen ... until I started to fucking want her.

"You listened to my conversation?" was her reply, her voice soft and sweet, drowsy and laced with the alcohol she'd consumed.

"I overheard."

A thick moment of silence stretched between us.

"I didn't tell her I'd go." She glanced out at the back yard, leaning against the banister so her upper body was almost parallel with the ground. "It's not really my scene, but you know Georgia," she said and looked at me then. "When she has her mind set on something..."

I shouldn't have stared at her ass. I shouldn't have pictured myself running my hands over those perfect globes, like the roundness of a peach. Fuck, I wanted to run my tongue between the crease in the center, wanted to spread the cheeks and stare at her perfectly pink pussy.

My mouth watered. My cock hardened.

Fuck.

I shifted on my feet, trying to hide the fact I was

getting harder than fucking steel.

"But maybe she's right," Ivy said, glancing at the back yard again. "I'm nineteen and should celebrate like I'm young and not some old lady not wanting to leave the house." She shrugged, as if talking to herself. Ivy pushed herself up, but I could see she was still unsteady on her feet, and when she went to push away from the banister, she almost lost her balance.

I was right there next to her a second later, my hand on her hip, steadying her, looking down at her as she glanced up at me with wide eyes. My fingers were curled tightly around her tiny tucked-in waist, my heart pounding, the scent of her getting me drunker than any liquor ever could.

I knew what I was about to ask was not my business. I was crossing lines as I held on to her, looked into her eyes. I couldn't help myself. "I bet all the guys at school are after you, aren't they, Ivy?" My voice was low, the alcohol making it sound even more husky, my arousal thickening it. I was still hard, and I prayed like hell she didn't glance down and see the way my jeans were tented.

She didn't say anything for a moment, but I could see the way her pulse was beating frantically at the base of her throat. She licked her lips, running her tongue along the bottom swell first and then bringing it up over the top.

God, I wanted her right then and there, wanted to cup the back of her head and kiss her, make her see that she was mine and nobody else could have her.

"Nobody's after me," she said so low it was almost a whisper.

She started breathing harder, and I glanced down at her hand, which was wrapped around the banister of the deck, and could see how tightly she held it. The desire poured off of her in waves, or maybe it was just wishful thinking on my part that I had this effect on her, that she wanted me as much as I wanted her.

"You're lying," I said and looked at her lips. My cock dug against the zipper of my jeans, demanding to be free. I bet she was so tight and pink between her legs, and would be so wet for me. "There's no way they're not after you, Ivy." My voice was nothing more than a guttural whisper at this point, the alcohol really moving through my bloodstream now, mixing with my arousal until I couldn't think straight, let alone stop this.

"Matthew." She whispered my name and I knew I was a fucking goner. There was no way I could control myself, not when she looked at me with desire in her eyes. Not when I could practically smell how wet she was between those pretty thighs of hers.

I knew one thing for certain ... if she gave herself to me, stopping this would be really fucking hard.

6

Ivy

God, was this really happening?

I'd meant to head back inside, maybe to sleep off the schnapps buzz, or maybe to get away from my intense feelings for Matthew. The way he looked at me, spoke to me, screamed possessiveness. Or maybe it was all in my head?

At least I had thought that until he put his hand on my waist to steady me, until he spoke low about guys at school wanting me. It was then I knew these feelings weren't just one-sided.

The alcohol had made my emotions more consuming, more heightened. I could hear my heart beating in my ears, feel it beating against my ribs. My mouth was dry, my throat tight. My nipples were hard, the wetness between my thighs having everything to do with the sight of Matthew.

His eyes were hooded, his gaze glossy. I could smell the whiskey on his breath and I swore I felt myself getting even drunker. I felt so buzzed, my face hot, my cheeks probably red. I could taste the peach liquor on my tongue, assumed he could smell it on my breath.

But still he said nothing.

"You shouldn't be drinking," he said.

No, I really should have, especially given what was happening right now.

"And neither should you," I responded, almost challenging him with my tone.

He placed his hands on the banister on either side of my body and leaned down slightly so he could look in my eyes. I averted my gaze, feeling the weight of his stare, of this moment crashing between us.

"Look at me, Ivy," he said softly but with a hint of command.

I couldn't breathe, didn't even know what was going on. This wasn't just Matthew being close to me. This was something much different, something much more.

Disobeying him wasn't even an option. I lifted my head and stared into his eyes. They were glossy in appearance, a little red-rimmed from the alcohol. Maybe I shouldn't feel aroused at a time like this, for a man like him, but my emotions were running rampant and I couldn't help myself.

For long moments we didn't speak, just stared at each other, the heat moving between us, my arousal becoming suffocating. I felt something shift in me, this boldness claiming me, the likes of which I'd never felt before.

Do it. Take control. Do what you've always wanted to.

The alcohol spoke loudly within me.

Without thinking, I moved in those last few inches until my lips pressed against his. For several long seconds neither of us moved, breathed. I didn't even think I could form a coherent thought in that moment. I expected him to move back, push me away. But instead our lips stayed connected. I felt, heard his breathing increase, but he didn't deepen the kiss as I desperately wanted ... needed.

I let my arousal and emotions lead me and pressed my lips firmer against his. Still he stayed still, didn't stop this, but also didn't progress it.

I parted my mouth and ran my tongue along his bottom lip. The soft groan that came from him gave me the confidence I needed.

God, this is really happening.

I opened my mouth even further and he followed suit. Excitement and shock filled me.

I was kissing Matthew, my *uncle* Matthew.

Our tongues touched and my pussy got wet instantly. I was soaked, so incredibly drenched in a matter of seconds that my panties started to feel uncomfortable as they rubbed against my sensitive flesh.

I felt bold in that moment, in the fact he wasn't stopping this. I placed my hands on his shoulders and pressed my chest against his. My breasts rubbed seductively against the hard muscles of his pecs, my nipples hardening even further. And then he groaned softly and tilted our heads at the same time, deepening the kiss. I couldn't help the small mewling sounds that came from me.

As if the noises I'd made had reality snapping back in place, Matthew pulled away. His breathing was erratic and his lips were red from our kiss. We stared at each other for several long moments. What would he do? What would I do?

He glanced at my lips, his gaze growing heavy-lidded.

I wanted more than another kiss. I wanted his naked body pressed against mine, wanted his hands on me, stroking, caressing ... pushing my thighs apart. I wanted to feel him settling between my legs, the erection I'd felt against my belly just moments before being pushed deep inside of me.

I reached for him again, but he shook his head

and moved away. Hurt and embarrassment slammed into me and I felt my face become hot as I stared at him.

"Matthew?" I whispered.

He shook his head and closed his eyes, the expression on his face seeming like he was in pain.

"I can't, Ivy. This isn't right."

My throat was so tight and dry, humiliation filling me. "But it feels right." The words spilled from me.

He stared at me, looking like he wanted to continue, like he wanted to say more, and here I was, my heart on my sleeve and the world falling away.

"It doesn't matter, Ivy." His voice was so deep, so gruff. "I'm your uncle."

"Step-uncle."

He shook his head again. "I've known you since you were a little girl, and wanting you the way I do, kissing you, touching you..." He moved away another foot and I felt on the verge of crying. "This whole situation is wrong on so many levels." He ran his hand over his jaw. "I'm taking advantage of you."

Shock filled me at his words.

Taking advantage of me?

Had I heard him right?

"But I want this. I want you, Matthew." I licked my lips. "I love you so much."

"Shit, Ivy. My sweet girl." He took a step toward me

and I sucked in a breath, thinking this might happen, he might be with me, tell me he loved me.

"I've wanted you since you turned eighteen. But my feelings for you aren't right. They cross lines."

We were still so close, but I was afraid to touch him. He looked down at my mouth and I thought he might kiss me, that he'd give in to these desires. But then this mask covered his face. He'd built that wall around himself, closed the door on this ... on us.

I was so embarrassed. How could I face him after this?

He kept his head down for a moment and then shifted to look at me.

"You don't want me." I said that as a phrase, not a question.

"It isn't that I..." He ran his hand over his jaw again before continuing. "It isn't that I don't want this, want you, Ivy." The way he looked at me was intense, but he was holding himself back.

"I want you too, Matthew," I said honestly.

He closed his eyes and made this deep sound in the back of his throat. When he opened them again, I could see there was pain hidden behind the dark depths.

"I want you, Ivy, so fucking much and that scares the shit out of me." A moment of silence passed between us as those words hung in the air. "But it's wrong to desire you. The relationships that would be ruined if I went through with my needs, my desires for you..." He didn't finish speaking, just shook his head and looked torn. "But despite all of that, knowing it's not right to touch you, think about you in the way I do, I can't stop the way I feel." He reached out and touched my cheek. "I love you. I'm in love with you." He smoothed his fingers along the curve of my jaw before running over the outline of my lips.

He looked at me like a man in love, like a man ... lost.

"I may not be able to stop the way I feel, but I can stop my actions, keep this from going any further than it already has."

And just like that, just with a few softly spoken words, my world crumbled around me.

————

Matthew

I was a fucking shitty person, an asshole brother, and there had to be something wrong with me for not only wanting my step-niece, but for crossing that line and kissing her.

I'd seen the look on her face when I walked away, when I stopped it all. She'd been so desperate for me, her love reflecting in her expression as she stared up at me with wide eyes, parted lips, and rosy cheeks.

She'd gotten that way because of me, because of how I make her feel.

And all I'd wanted to do was pull her in close again and devour her mouth, slide my tongue into the warm, sweet recesses between her lips, and make her see that she was only mine. I didn't want her with anyone else, even if being with her wasn't something that I could ever have. I was a selfish bastard, and could see myself beating some asshole to the ground for even looking in her direction.

I exhaled and stopped in the middle of my room, breathing out roughly again as I lifted my hand and ran it over the back of my head. Shit, I'd have to jerk off in the shower, relieve this massive hard-on I was sporting because the fucker just wouldn't go down. Then again, it was as if it had a mind of its own, as if he knew the ultimate pleasure was just in the next room and that's the only thing that could sate the bastard.

"Fuck," I said harshly, but kept my voice low. Not only was Stephan going through his own shit and needed me to be strong for everyone, but I'd just gone and kissed his daughter. I'd just gone and staked my claim on her. And as much as I knew that being with her was not something I could possibly fucking do, every single part of my being was roaring out for me to keep her, no matter what.

I was at war with myself, even as every single part of me was saying that there was no fucking way I'd give her up.

7

Matthew

"You'll be gone for two weeks?"

I glanced over at Ivy, hearing the concern in her voice. It was just her and her dad, had been since her mom passed away.

He'd never been away from her this long, and I could see that she was nervous about it.

"As of right now, although I could be home sooner, or it might be a little later." He gave her a sad smile. "But I need this, sweetheart. Without a stable job the bills are going to start stacking up."

"I can get a part time job and help," she said instantly.

"No," Stephan said.

"Absolutely not," I said right after he spoke. They

both looked at me but I kept my composure. "Focus on school. I'm here and will help your dad out. Everything will be fine." She stared at me for a long moment. I swallowed, my throat so fucking tight at the very thought that we'd be here alone.

That was dangerous. Really fucking dangerous.

I needed to keep my damn distance. I needed to be a good brother, a good man. And being with Ivy, going after her and making her mine, would have me crossing so many fucking lines there would be no going back.

It's already too late.

Those words slammed into my head repeatedly, refusing to back the hell down. I pushed away from the doorframe and walked farther into the kitchen. Stephan was sitting at the table, this sympathetic look on his face as he stared at Ivy.

"Honey, this is the first real job I've had since everything happened. It might only be temporary, but right now it's all I have." He smiled at her and it broke my fucking heart seeing my big brother like this.

He'd always been so strong, so in control of everything. Even after his wife had passed away, I'd never seen a man have his shit as much together as he did. But right now, he looked lost, and I knew that was because of his job, but also because of the conflict he felt was going on between his personal life and his home life.

I knew he wanted Ivy to meet the woman he was seeing. I knew he wanted everything to be good between them. Maybe he thought she saw him differently because of it all. But that's not what I saw.

I saw it in her face, saw the way she looked at him. She loved him no matter what, unconditionally. And that was one of the reasons I'd fallen in love with her.

That was one of the reasons I fell so hard for her.

"It just seems like such a long time, and you'll be so far away."

"It's just a couple states away. It'll be done and over with before you know it." He looked up at me then and smiled. "I'm just glad Matthew is here to handle things and take care of you. I don't think I could have left you alone." A moment of silence passed. "I know you're an adult and all, but I would've been too worried." He stood up and pulled Ivy off the chair to give her a hug. "I have to pack, though. I've got to head out soon so I can drive through the night and get there in the morning."

Ivy nodded and pulled back. Damn, she was so strong. After everything that was going on, what she'd been through with losing her mom, she kept her shit together. She was smart, an honor student, had the pick of where she wanted to go for college, and I was so damn proud of her even if I didn't say it.

Stephan gave us both one more look, then started to walk past me. He stopped and clapped me on the back.

"Thank you again. For everything."

God, I felt like such a fucking bastard. The memory of the kiss I'd shared with Ivy was so fresh in my mind, so fucking fresh that I felt my lips tingle, felt the arousal rush through my veins. My desire started climbing and I couldn't help but look at her.

Stephan left the kitchen and I stood there staring at her. She glanced up at me as if she could feel my gaze. I had no doubt she could. It was like she was on autopilot, like she knew she had to be a rock for everyone around her even if it slowly chipped away at her.

"This is weird, right?" she finally said and sat back down at the table.

I clenched my jaw tightly. God, she was beautiful as she stared up at me with her big blue eyes. "How do you mean?"

She didn't speak for a long moment, but finally shrugged. "I guess how things play out, how life works." She was staring at me, and I wanted nothing more than to pick her up and carry her to my room, lay her on my bed and just hold her. "I would have never thought my mom would die so young. I would have never thought my dad would lose his job because he fell in love with a woman so much younger than him." She shrugged again. "Life is just funny, I guess."

"It's unpredictable." My voice was colder. I didn't want to sound so hard.

She nodded. "Yeah, that's a good word for it."

The silence descended again, and I knew that I had to be strong, had to be someone she looked up to, not someone she desired. I was in love with her, and that would never change, but I had to stay away.

And I knew that as much as I wanted her, as much as I told myself that I couldn't let her go, I had to keep away.

She was a temptation that I didn't know if I could resist.

She was a drug that fed my addiction.

She was the one woman I loved and knew I'd never fully have.

And the very thought of staying away was like someone had reached in and torn out my fucking heart.

But it was for the best. Right?

It had to be because pain this fucking intense had to be for something.

8

Ivy

I watched Matthew walk out of the kitchen twenty minutes ago, and yet here I sat, staring at the wall, thinking about everything that had happened this far.

To be honest, it was pretty minuscule in the grand scheme of things.

So what, I was in love with a man I couldn't really have.

So what, my father was seeing a woman close to my age.

Things were always the worst before they got better, right? I wanted to be the adult I legally was, the one who could stand on her own two feet, who was starting college in the fall. I wanted to show everyone I could handle things on my own, that I didn't need babysitters, that I could help support this family.

But stress ate away at a person, and there was enough of that going around right now.

I found myself standing and leaving the kitchen, walking up the stairs and heading toward my father's room at the end of the hall. The door was slightly open and I knocked on it, pushing on it slightly so I could see inside.

My dad had a suitcase on the bed, and a stack of clothes beside that. There was a pile of hangers in the center of the mattress, and his loafers on the floor. He stood by the closet and glanced over at me, smiling. He was just pulling out a dress shirt when he turned to face me.

"Everything okay, Ivy?"

I swallowed, my throat so thick. I didn't even know if this was the best time, but I figured there was no point in waiting. Maybe if I was honest—about this at least—it would take away some of that stress.

"I just wanted to tell you that I'm happy you're happy." There was a long moment of silence between us, and I felt the air change, felt something in my father shift.

He'd been taken aback by what I said.

"I just wanted to let you know that I don't think it's weird that you're seeing someone close to my age. I'm not upset, and I'm not fragile. And I think you feel that way because you haven't really talked about her, or any of this with me, to be honest." I took a deep breath in. "But if you're happy, I'm happy. And I just wanted you to know that before you left."

He walked toward me, and in the process tossed the shirt he'd taken out of the closet onto the bed. He took my hands in his and gave them a light squeeze.

"I'll be honest, Ivy. It wasn't me losing my job that had me so worried. Even me leaving for this job didn't weigh on me so heavily." He licked his lips and looked down at our conjoined hands. "It's the fact that I felt like I've disappointed you." He looked up at me then and I stared into his blue eyes, ones that were exactly like mine. "It's been so long since I cared about anyone. After your mother passed away I focused on raising you. That's what mattered. But this just kind of ... happened. And I am happy. But your happiness matters to me as well, even more than my own."

God, if only I could be honest about how I felt for Matthew. "Your happiness is just as important as anybody else's. And I know Mom wouldn't want you to be alone. I know I don't want you to be." I smiled at him and gave his hands a squeeze.

"I know Cora is young, just a year older than you, but I think you'd really like her. I hope you do."

This was the first time he'd ever said her name. It

was a little bit strange hearing my father talk about a woman he cared for. But it was only that way because I'd never seen him love anyone but my mother.

"I love you, Dad. I don't care that you're dating Cora. I know that has been weighing heavily on you."

He let go of my hands and smiled. "It's a little weird though, isn't it?"

I chuckled softly and nodded. "It's a lot weird, if I'm being honest. But like I said, I'm not a child and don't need to be sheltered. If you're happy, then I'm happy." I ran my hands down my thighs, my jeans feeling extra rough against the sensitive flesh. "I'd like to meet her. I'd like to meet the woman you care about."

He gave me another smile and this one was more genuine, more from the heart.

"Okay," he said softly. "I'd like you to meet her." He pulled me in for another hug.

I rested my head on his chest, listening to the steady rhythm of his heart. I remembered doing this as a child, that sound lulling me to sleep, telling me that everything would be all right because my father was here. He was my protector, looked out for me, and made sure I never went to bed upset. He held me as I cried after my mother passed away, told me everything would be okay because he'd make it so.

And as I pulled back and looked into his face, I knew even at nineteen years old I was still my father's little girl. I knew no matter what, he'd love me, even if I told him I was in love with Matthew ... his brother.

I left my father so he could finish packing and headed to my room. I closed the door and leaned against it, resting my head back on the wood and closing my eyes.

It had only been a few days since Matthew and I had shared that kiss, yet in just those few days he'd been avoiding me, had been distant, almost even cold to me. I wanted to believe he thought he was doing the right thing. I wanted to believe that what he'd told me after he'd pressed his body to mine had been what he'd really meant.

Surely those words weren't a heat of the moment kind of thing?

But this was all new territory for me. And each day I felt him building that wall thicker between us, my heart broke a little more.

I could either accept it and try and move on, or stand my ground and refuse to give up on the only man I'd ever loved.

Because the very thought of almost having Matthew, but then realizing it might never come to fruition, felt as though a piece of me had been pulled away, as if I'd been ripped in half. And the more he pulled back, the more I wanted him, the more I wanted to admit that what we had was good and right and everything in-between.

But the memory of him stopping, of him saying we couldn't do this, that it was wrong, replayed in my head like a broken record.

Part of me knew he was right, that being together would start this butterfly effect, this ripple in the water that could very well turn into a tidal wave. I didn't want to hurt my father. I didn't want to hurt anyone. I just wanted to be with Matthew and love him and not have to worry about what everyone else might say.

Because if it felt right, if I knew being with Matthew was how it was supposed to be, it couldn't be wrong, right?

9

Matthew

I heard her come in, the sound of her setting her book bag on the ground seeming overly loud.

I stood by the kitchen sink, my hands wrapped around the edge, staring out the window at the half-constructed gazebo Stephan had started but hadn't yet finished. My body was tense, the need to go to her strong. But I held my ground, stayed away.

It had been days since Stephan had left for his temp job, and I had made myself scarce, working extra hours, but ensuring sure I was home every night so Ivy wasn't alone. She might be an adult, but that didn't mean I couldn't make sure she was safe, make sure she wasn't alone.

There was a moment where I heard her walking

toward the kitchen, but then she stopped. I wondered if she was coming in. It wasn't like I'd been very friendly the past few days, not since the kiss, not since I told myself I needed to try and keep my distance.

I looked over my shoulder, expecting her to be standing in the doorway, but it was empty. And then I heard the stairs creaking as she went up. My stomach clenched, the need to go to her so fucking strong.

Fuck.

I closed my eyes and faced forward again, knowing I needed to figure out what the fuck I was going to do because this wasn't working. Living under the same roof as Ivy was torture. Not being able to touch her was painful. And lying about how I felt was driving me crazy.

I didn't know how long I stood there, staring at that gazebo, thinking about what the hell I was going to do. But it was the sound of the pipes rattling, and then Ivy screaming that had me propelling myself for the stairs. I took them two at a time, heard her down the hall, and raced into the bathroom and saw what had caused the issue.

Water sprayed from the faucet, drenching Ivy. Her mouth was open and her arms were out, as if she couldn't believe what was happening, that she was soaking wet.

The front of her was drenched, the white material

of her shirt sticking to her body. I lost my breath as I
stared at her, as I saw the way the fabric formed to her
breasts, sticking to them like a second skin. Her
nipples were hard, the water no doubt ice cold. I
could easily see the dark circles of her areolas.

Motherfucker.

I felt my entire body tighten painfully, my cock
hardening. I reached out and curled my hand around
the door frame, hearing it creak from the force. And all
I could do was stand there and stare at her as water
sprayed everywhere, our focus on each other.

"Matthew?" she asked in this small voice, as if she
were torn between the situation with the faucet and
with me standing there transfixed by the sight of her.

But then I snapped to attention and forced myself
to leave her, to go to the basement and shut off the
water. I took a moment to just stand there, bracing my
hands on my thighs as I bent over and just breathed
out, my eyes closed and trying to rein in my control.

I only stood there for a few moments, telling myself
that I could control this lust. I could control myself. I
headed back upstairs, grabbing the toolbox on my way,
and gripped the banister of the stairs as I stepped onto
the upper landing. I looked down the hallway but
couldn't see Ivy. That was probably best. As I walked
toward the bathroom, I passed her bedroom, the door
slightly open. I don't know why I glanced inside,

maybe hoping to see her, maybe being filled with some sick, masochistic desire to see what I couldn't have.

But then I froze, my body hardening as I saw her through the slightly ajar door. She had her shirt off, her smooth, perfect back in view, her skin this peachy color, the slight indentation of her spine running down the center having my mouth watering.

I saw the image of me on my knees behind her, my hands gripping her hips, my forehead resting on the center of her back. I could practically smell the soap on her skin, this sweet fragrance that came from her. I could picture myself running the tip of my nose up the length of her spine before following that trail with my tongue.

This deep groan left me before I could stop it, and she looked over her shoulder, her eyes widening as she saw me standing there.

Fuck.

I shut my eyes, placing that wall between us again, feeling my face harden, my expression go cold. Her eyes widened even further and I knew it wasn't because of the surprise of me standing there, but because of the change in my demeanor. I turned before I could make things worse, or I could ruin anything. Once in the bathroom I shut the door, locking myself in there, and putting an extra barricade between Ivy and me.

I was so fucking far gone, so lost in the reality of this all. And I knew that if I was going to be here, I had to be honest with Stephan. I could fight this with myself, force myself to stay away, but what I felt for Ivy would never go away. It would never dim. It would just keep growing until it festered within me and I fucking snapped.

I stared at myself in the mirror, the man who looked back at me seeming tortured. But then again, I was.

I knew I couldn't keep this up, couldn't stop myself. There'd be a point in time, probably sooner rather than later, where I just said *fuck it* and claimed her.

There'd be a point where I couldn't stay away from Ivy. There'd be a point where I made her mine.

Fuck the repercussions.

10

Ivy

I was adjusting my shirt when I stepped off the landing and ran right into Matthew's chest. A soft sound escaped me and I stumbled back, gripping the banister in the process. But he already had his hand on my upper arm, his big, strong fingers curled around my skin, searing me to the bone.

I sucked in a breath and glanced up at him, his muscular body so powerful and big he blocked out everything else behind him. I saw nothing but him.

Over the last couple of days, we'd kept our distance from each other, mainly because he was working a lot of hours and I was focusing on school. And he was all I thought of.

But I knew that it wasn't just our schedules that

created this wedge between us. I knew he was working extra hours so we didn't have to talk about what had happened between us, so he could avoid me and not deal with the reality of the situation. I could see it in the way he looked at me, felt it in the way the air changed when he was near.

He stared at me for long seconds, not moving, his hand staying on my upper arm. I knew why he was keeping his distance, knew it was because of the taboo aspect of all of this. But then again, I didn't know why he was stopping this. I could see the way he looked at me, especially right now, with his gaze heavy lidded and the air around us electrically charged.

The desire he had for me was clear, as strong and powerful as mine. But still he said nothing, just watched me as if he were a predator and I was his prey.

"Heading out." He didn't phrase it like a question. He knew where I was going tonight, had told me he'd overheard the party comment by Georgia.

I nodded, licked my lips, and took a step back, seemingly all in the same breath. And still he stayed close, still he kept his hand on me. A long moment passed before he finally let go, moved back a step, and shoved his hands in his pockets. His body was so big and powerful, the tattoos covering his golden skin having every feminine part of my body coming alive.

"Where's the party at?" His voice was hard, cold.

I felt chills race over my body just from the sound of it. It was as if he was in parental mode. That's how protective he sounded right now.

"At a guy's house we go to school with."

He was silent. Still.

"A guy?"

I nodded.

"I think you should stay home. I know exactly how guys act at parties, and I'm assuming there'll be alcohol there, which makes it even worse."

As much as I loved Matthew, and wanted to be with him, the hardness that surrounded him now, the way he pushed me away, had this anger slowly filling me.

I shook his hold off and narrowed my eyes. "I'm not a child. I'm going to this party." He made a low, gruff sound, almost a growl of disapproval.

I pushed past him toward the front door.

"Ivy, I'm serious."

I stopped and curled my hands into fists at my sides, turning and facing him. There was so much I wanted to say, but now wasn't the time. Instead, I tipped my chin up and looked him right in the eyes. "Matthew, you're not my father. I'm going to this party and I'll be home later. I'll be fine." His face grew hard, authoritative. He could be pissed all he wanted. "You don't get to tell me what the hell to do." I swallowed, my anger mixing with my emotions. "You don't get to kiss me then push me away and think you care about how I feel, what I do."

The expression that covered his face tightened my chest. He looked like I'd just ripped his heart out.

I heard the sound of a car pulling into the driveway, and knew it was Georgia here to pick me up.

Thank God she had perfect timing.

I could see that Matthew wanted to argue the point, maybe demand I stay. He'd always been protective of me, but right now seemed different. He seemed more intense, dominating.

I gave him one more last lingering look before turning and stepping out the front door. The truth was, it was hard leaving him. I wanted to stay there, wanted to talk, work things out. But if this was how my life was supposed to go, without Matthew in it, then I needed to try and move forward.

He made his stance clear, silently told me that we couldn't be together.

I had to respect that.

I had to accept it.

What other choice did I have?

11

Ivy

Georgia pulled up to the party, cars lined up on either side of the road, a row filling the driveway. We had to park down the street because it was clear the place was congested and we wouldn't find anything closer to Zachary's house.

His place was on the outskirts of town, more like a farmhouse than anything else, although there wasn't anything "farm" about the estate. Zachary came from old money and his house portrayed that.

Because of who his family was, and because the house was so far away from town, this party would be pretty untouchable.

Georgia parked and cut the engine and we just sat there. A truck drove by, four guys in the back of the pickup, one standing up and banging his hand on the roof of the vehicle. They all hooted and hollered, beer cans in their hands, and a keg situated between them.

"Georgia, are you sure this is a good idea? This seems pretty wild and it's still really early." I looked at her and could see her worrying her bottom lip, maybe thinking about changing her mind.

But then she looked at me and grinned. "This is going to be the party we won't forget."

I looked at the house. I had no doubt about that.

She climbed out and then opened the back passenger door, pulling out a medium-size paper bag that looked like it had some heft to it. I knitted my brows in confusion.

"What's that?"

She opened the bag and pulled out a wine cooler, wagging her brows.

"Got seven more where this came from."

I could have snorted for how proud she sounded about that. Wine coolers compared to what was probably flowing. Her party was tame as hell.

"Let me guess, friend of a friend got that for you too?" She winked and slammed the door shut.

I climbed out, making sure my phone was tucked into my pocket. I breathed out as I stared up the hill to where the house was located.

"Hey, you never told me how that peach schnapps

was." I looked over at her and grimaced. That had her chuckling. "That bad?"

I felt my cheeks heat at the thought of what had happened after I'd drunk all the schnapps. "Let's just say I don't wanna talk about it."

She grabbed my hand and together we walked up the hill.

"Fair enough."

The noise got louder the closer we got, and although I wasn't a prude when it came to parties, this seemed a little out of control already.

We saw a few people we went to school with, who I considered friends, and we all started heading inside together. The lights were bright, the music loud, and this hazy film filled the entire interior of the house. I could smell a hint of weed, the aroma of alcohol. It all coated the air, wrapping around me and pulling me in like a temptation.

Although I wasn't a big drinker, and certainly didn't do drugs, when you were in this kind of situation everything seemed a little bit unreal. It felt dreamlike, that you could do just about anything and it would be okay ... it would be safe.

I heard some shouting and looked to my right to see Zachary and a group of guys start to head over. They pushed their way through the thick sea of people, beer bottles and cans in their hands, their glossy expressions and red-rimmed eyes telling me they were already pretty drunk.

Zachary came up to stand beside Georgia. Marcus, Charlie, and Lane were next. They all looked trashed with glazed-over expressions and goofy grins on their faces.

"You guys came," Zachary said with a big grin on his face, flashing straight white teeth.

I looked around the living room, bodies packed inside like sardines. "Zach, this is kind of intense." All the guys started laughing and I looked back at them. I saw the way Georgia glanced at Charlie, and for the first time I noticed the desire and longing in her expression. Had I been blind this whole time? It was clear she wanted him, but Charlie on the other hand seemed oblivious. Or maybe he wanted her too and I was just as blind to that fact.

"Yeah, it's bigger than what we thought," Zach said and looked over at his friends. They started laughing obnoxiously again and I was starting to think this might not have been a good idea coming here. This really wasn't my scene. I was more of a bookworm, a stay-at-home kind of girl who wanted to be covered in a blanket watching some old romance on TV.

"Here, Ivy," Marcus said and handed me a beer. I smiled, taking it but not really having any desire for it. For the next twenty minutes, I stood there nursing the beer until it got warm and started to make my stomach turn.

"Girl, are you still sipping on that one?" Zachary said and tipped the bottle up to my mouth. "Drink up, we got another one for ya." Before I could say anything, warm liquid was rolling down my throat. He took the empty bottle and handed me a shot.

"Listen up everyone," Marcus hollered. There was still music pounding but a moment later it lowered. "We got a birthday to celebrate." Marcus tipped his chin in my direction. "Baby girl here just turned nineteen. We got a special birthday shot for her." He held up the shot. "A buttery nipple."

The crowd started hollering and shouting, cheering me on. Zachary gestured for me to take the shot from Marcus, and with everyone watching me I felt my face heat. The shot was this creamy coffee color with whipped cream on the top. It looked more like a dessert than anything else. How bad could it be if it looked so good?

I took the shot and smelled it. It was sweet, and I couldn't really pick up on the strong aroma of liquor.

"Shot. Shot. Shot."

The crowd yelled and hollered.

I tossed the shot back, the flavor of butterscotch instantly coating my mouth.

I hated butterscotch.

Zachary took the shot glass away and everybody started cheering. They acted like I'd just done a keg stand or something. I breathed out through the burn of alcohol, surprised that it was a hell of a lot stronger than I'd assumed. Someone handed me another beer and I took a long sip, trying to get rid of the nasty flavor in my mouth. I needed to slow down, to pace myself.

"Water," I all but shouted to Georgia. She nodded and took my hand, pulling me toward the kitchen. I moved to the side as she pushed her way through the people and grabbed two bottles of water off the counter. My stomach felt queasy from the beer then taking the shot.

When she handed me one of the bottles, I cracked the cap and took a long drink. For the rest of the night I was sticking with water. Last thing I needed was to get drunk again, go home and run into Matthew, then deal with a hangover the next morning.

"Come on, let's actually enjoy this party." Georgia looped her arm through mine and grinned, leading us back into the living room.

Zachary and the other guys were in the process of bringing a keg into the house, metal clanging against pieces of furniture and the floor as they maneuvered it through the crowd of people and finally set it down in the center of the room.

It was like I was at a concert, people shouting and

yelling, dancing and groping each other. I had no doubt there were people banging upstairs, in the bathrooms, hell, probably even right around the corner. I could practically smell the scent of sex filling the air.

And maybe at my age I should have been enjoying the party, making out with some random guy in the corner, getting felt up by one of the jocks. But instead I felt like a loner, an outcast. I felt like I didn't belong, like where I should be was back at home, curled up on the couch and pressed up against Matthew, his arm around me and not a care in the world ... least of all what people thought about a niece being in love with her uncle.

12

Matthew

I paced the kitchen, not caring if I was going to eventually leave a rut in the floor.

I brought the bottle of beer to my mouth and took a long drink, glancing out the window at the driveway where my truck was.

Reaching into my pocket and pulling out my cell, I stared at it. I wanted to go to her. It would be easy enough to find her, to make a few calls and see where she was. The town we lived in was small, and word spread around, especially if it was concerning a big-ass high school party.

But I didn't want to break her trust. I didn't want to embarrass her by making a scene, and I sure as fuck would.

What I wanted to do was find out where she was. I wanted to pull her out of that house and throw her over my shoulder, tell her I was doing this for her own good.

Then I'd bring her home, take her to my bed, and finally claim her. I'd part her pretty thighs, stare at the sweet spot between them, and devour her.

Fuck, I was hard thinking about her, picturing all the filthy fucking things I wanted to do to Ivy.

And trying to refrain myself any more seemed fruitless.

———

Ivy

Two hours later I was staring at Georgia as she stumbled around.

"Georgia, you're trashed," I said and helped her into the bathroom.

"Ugh, I know," she slurred and sank to her knees. "I need to make myself throw up so I'll feel better."

I grabbed the long fall of her hair and kept it out of the way as she tried to do just that. After a few minutes of dry heaving, she sighed and leaned back.

"Why did you drink so much?" I asked her.

She had her arms braced on the toilet seat and turned her head to look at me, her eyes unfocused.

"Why did you let me drink so much?" She started giggling and then promptly groaned.

Although the truth was I'd paced myself for the past couple hours, Georgia had been the total opposite. Where I was completely sober, Georgia was piss-ass trashed. Every time I'd seen her, she was weaving in and out of the crowd, with either a beer in hand or a shot. Not to mention, Charlie was the one by her side the whole time, being her drinking dealer.

And I was pretty sure that's why she just kept chugging them back ... because Charlie was the one guy she clearly desperately wanted.

"Ugh, Ivy." She looked up at me, her eyes watery, her cheeks red. "I need to go home."

I nodded and helped her up. "Let's go." We started heading out of the bathroom and down the stairs, Georgia hanging on to me as her balance was for shit. "Your mom isn't home, right?"

She shook her head. "Working third shift."

Good. Last thing she needed was her mom seeing her drunk.

I had my focus on her and ended up tripping over my own feet on the last step. Hands caught my shoulders, steadying me, and I glanced up to see Marcus standing there, a grin on his face.

"Easy there." He let go of me and looked at Georgia. "Shit, she's gone, isn't she?"

"Yeah." I held my hand out to her. Georgia dug in her pocket and tossed her keys on my palm. "I'm gonna take her home." I looked back at Marcus.

"She drove?" I nodded. "How are you getting her home after dropping her off?"

"Shit," I muttered. "I hadn't thought of that."

"It's cool. I'm heading out anyway." He moved to the side for us. "I can follow you guys then take you home."

"Really?" That sounded a lot better than having to call Matthew to come get me, especially after everything and how awkward things had become. "That would be awesome, thanks." Marcus smiled at me and in the back of my mind I thought about what Georgia had said. How he was interested in me.

The thing was, I didn't see Marcus as anything more than a friend. We'd gone to middle school together and were in our last year of high school together. He was attractive and popular, was an overall nice guy, but his reputation as a playboy wasn't something I was into.

He pushed people out of the way as I helped Georgia to the front door, and then we made our way down the street toward where her car was parked.

Marcus had parked closer to the house, and by the

time I got Georgia in the passenger side seat and buckled in, then climbed into the driver's seat, he was coming down the road. He slowed his car when he got to me and I rolled down my window.

"I'll follow you," he said and grinned.

"Are you sure you're okay to drive?" The low sound of music pumping from his stereo could be heard.

"I'm good. I stopped drinking hours ago. I shouldn't have even come out tonight. I have a track meet tomorrow."

A part of me wished I could be attracted to Marcus.

It certainly would have made things a lot easier in my life.

13

Ivy

Marcus pulled his car up to the curb in front of my house. I looked up at it, no lights on, the place looking abandoned. I didn't assume Matthew was in bed. No doubt he was waiting up for me.

I shifted on the seat and smiled at Marcus. "Thanks for taking me home." After I'd gotten Georgia inside, tucked her in bed, and locked up when I left, Marcus had been waiting. I'd found out he lived close to Zachary, in the rich part of town, and following me to Georgia's then going to my house meant he'd gone out of his way twice.

"Hey, it's no problem."

I opened the door and climbed out, realizing

Marcus was getting out as well. Looking over my shoulder, I felt my brows knit.

"I was just gonna walk you to the front door. Looks like no one's home, and it's late as fuck. I'd feel like a real asshole if I didn't make sure you got in safely instead of sitting my ass in the car and not being a gentleman."

I couldn't help but chuckle, and didn't bother telling him he really didn't have to go to the trouble. "Thank you."

We headed up to the porch, and when I stood by the front door I faced him. "Thanks for everything, Marcus. It was really nice of you."

"No trouble." He shifted, looking a little uncomfortable, and I felt confusion fill me.

"You okay?"

He'd averted his gaze for a moment, but now looked at me. The expression he wore spoke volumes.

Oh.

He was going to try and kiss me.

"Um," I said and turned to face the front door, getting ready to unlock it. A kiss from Marcus wasn't what I wanted or needed, even if he was a nice guy. "I better get inside."

Before I could open the door, I felt him move a step closer. I looked at him and saw him smile.

"I see you a lot at school, but we don't talk very much," he said.

I swallowed, feeling his desire for me pretty intense at the moment.

"I like you, Ivy. I'd like to get to know you a lot better. Maybe we can go out sometime?"

He reached out to maybe touch my arm, or pull me in close for that kiss, but before I could stop him, and before he made contact, the porch light turned on, and the front door swung open almost violently.

I snapped my head in that direction, feeling my eyes widen as I saw Matthew standing there. His big body took up the entire entryway, the shadows from inside the house, coupled with the muted light from overhead, making him seem almost ominous.

And his focus was right on Marcus.

"Whoa," Marcus said and took a step back, chuckling a little awkwardly. "You're a big guy." He looked between me and Matthew, and I could see the discomfort on his face.

Matthew took a step out, his body so massive he commanded everything. He was shirtless, and the tattoos that covered his chest and arms, creeping up his neck, made him look even more dangerous.

And still his focus was on Marcus.

"It's time for you to come inside, Ivy," Matthew said

without taking his gaze off of Marcus. "And it's time for you to go home, son."

I glanced at Marcus, feeling uncomfortable with how tense the situation had become. Matthew was pissed, that was clear, and the dominance he threw off right now, as if he were trying to show Marcus that he was the alpha, was tangible.

"Um," Marcus said and glanced at me a little nervously. "I guess I'll see you at school?" He gave me an awkward smile, glanced at Matthew once more, and then walked away.

I stood there for a moment just watching him, saw him get into his car, and then pull away. I could feel Matthew's gaze on me, like this heavy hand on my shoulder. I faced him, tipping my head back so I could look into his face. The shadows still concealed him, and the expression he wore was one I'd never seen before.

He seemed upset, but I also saw ... need.

I didn't say anything as I took a step forward. He moved to the side to allow me entrance, and when he shut the front door, we were submerged in darkness.

There was a lot I wanted to say, but right now probably wasn't the best time.

With one lingering look over my shoulder at him, barely making out his presence because of how dark the interior of the house was, I faced forward again. As

I went up the stairs, I felt his gaze on me, following me, watching me the entire time. And when I was in my room with the door shut, I leaned against it and just breathed.

But all I wanted to do was go right back down there and throw myself into his arms.

———————

Matthew

Possessiveness.

Jealousy.

Deep.

Unrequited rage.

I'd felt all of those things tenfold as I watched the little asshole walk Ivy up to the front door, as I heard him make his move on her, as I knew he'd try and kiss her.

I wasn't having any of that. No, fuck that.

And so I'd acted like some kind of spurned lover, some jealous boyfriend.

If anybody was going to have Ivy in all ways, it was going to be me. If anybody was going to know what she tasted like, felt like, sounded like as she moaned out pleasure, it would be me.

Only me.

I watched her walk up the stairs, could tell she was nervous, unsure of the situation. Hell, I was unsure of the situation. Because in that moment, as I saw her with another guy, the thoughts and images of them being together slamming in my head, the very idea that Ivy wouldn't be mine had totally thrown every fucking bit of self-control and rational thought I had out the window.

I couldn't stay away.

I wouldn't.

I'd have Ivy as mine, and fuck if it ruined everything.

14

Ivy

I put the clean set of pajamas on the counter and shut the bathroom door, staring at myself in the mirror. My body felt ultrasensitive, the memory of the kiss I'd shared with Matthew still so fresh in my mind, on my lips. My mouth tingled, my body reacted. All it took was that memory to ignite me.

I turned on the shower and waited for it to heat up, then got in, hoping the hot water might stave off some of this arousal burning within me.

But the longer I stayed under the spray, the more my desire for him grew. And what a fucking shame that was, seeing as I wouldn't ever be with him. He'd made that clear, told me we couldn't be together. And I understood him, but I hated it. It felt like someone had ripped my heart from me.

I shut off the water and stood there a moment, just letting the droplets slide down my body, the chill settle over my skin. Finally, I stepped out, dried off, and dressed, the clothing rubbing along my ultrasensitive skin, heightening my lust even further.

How I wished I could be with Matthew, that I could at least talk to someone about how I felt. But telling anyone my feelings would be met with condemnation, disgust, judgment. No, I couldn't even tell Georgia how I felt. I couldn't admit it to anyone.

I stared at myself in the mirror, the glass foggy, my reflection distorted. I lifted my hand to clear off the fog. I stared at myself for a second, feeling defeated, alone, and like a part of myself was missing.

I opened the bathroom door, the built-up steam billowing out in this cloud in front of me.

I could hear sounds from downstairs. I knew Matthew was just right below. Maybe if I went down there and demanded he stop hiding his feelings, he'd be with me. Or maybe I'd make a bigger fool of myself. Maybe I'd make things worse. And then I saw the light downstairs go off, heard him coming closer to the stairs. My heart started racing and I wanted to go to my room, to rush away, escape.

I was nervous, scared to see him. Things had gotten

so weird since the kiss, since he'd told me how he felt, and I to him. It was like he'd shut me out. It was when I heard the creak of the stairs and knew Matthew was coming up, that I found myself finally going to my room. But once I was there, I didn't shut the door. I left it cracked, the darkness from the lack of light, the humidity and scent of the body wash I'd used filling the air.

His room was right beside mine. He'd have to walk past my door to get to it, so when he was only a few feet away, I took a step back and held my breath. The door was still cracked, a small sliver of muted blue light from the window coming through.

And then I saw him. He didn't move past my door, and instead stopped, looking in my direction. Could he see me? Could he hear my heart racing?

I took a step back as he came forward one. My heart was racing, my palms sweating. My body was hot then cold, repeating over and over again. Dizziness slammed into me as I saw him right there, pushing my door open. The shadows and moonlight spilled into my room.

"You should be in bed," he said gruffly, his voice low, almost inaudible. "It's late."

I didn't say anything. I couldn't.

He leaned against the doorframe. "I'm sorry about earlier."

All I could do was nod.

"But I'm done fighting this."

Oh. God.

He pushed himself away from the door and came toward me. He stopped when he was just a foot from where I stood, his massive body making me feel so small and feminine.

"I don't trust myself around you, and so I've stayed away." A wall of hard, warm muscle pressed up against my chest and a gasp left me. My vision had adjusted to the darkness, and I could see his gaze on me, the fact he had this heavy-lidded expression. The smell of him, the feel of his chest pressed against mine reminded me all too well of what I really wanted, of who was right in front of me.

Desire rushed inside of me.

"Ivy." He said my name on a harsh groan, the scent of the alcohol he'd clearly been drinking lacing his breath. But it was like an aphrodisiac that heightened my hunger for him.

His hands were gently wrapped around my upper arms, keeping me balanced, yet drawing me closer to him.

I swallowed the lump in my throat. We didn't speak, just stared at each other, the darkness wrapping around us like a blanket that blocked out everything, everyone. My lips were suddenly dry and my heart thundered. I licked them again, my mouth tingling as I thought about that kiss we'd shared, as I imagined doing it over and over again.

I felt myself fall deeper and deeper into the web of arousal. Did he feel that unexplainable pull?

"What's going on?" I whispered. Whatever it was I didn't want it to end. I wanted it to go further.

He said nothing, just watched me. And then I watched him lower his head.

Oh, God. Kiss me, Matthew. Take me.

His lips were now a hairbreadth away from mine. The smell of whiskey swirled around me and seemed to make me intoxicated as well. That one beer and shot I'd had at the party had nothing on the smell of the liquor he'd drunk, on how it made me feel.

"God, Ivy ... how I feel about you."

How he felt about me? I couldn't breathe, felt lightheaded, my desire like a living entity inside of me.

"It consumes me. Confuses me." He swallowed, his Adams apple working. "I want you for myself. The very thought of another guy talking to you, touching you, shit, even looking at you makes me want to fucking tear him apart." He closed his eyes for a second, and when he opened them again, I got lost in the dark depths, in my feelings for him. "I love you, Ivy. I love you so fucking much it hurts to think of you not in my life. To think of you as not mine."

He lifted his hand and cupped my cheek, his palms big and warm, the calluses on his fingers from the hard manual labor he did making me feel feminine, soft.

"I tried to stay away, to keep my distance, but it's too fucking hard, Ivy. I'm going crazy not having you, not making it known you're mine."

I sucked in a breath, wanting to say so much but the words failing me.

He smoothed his thumb along my cheek. "It's wrong to want you, my brother's daughter, my niece."

I swallowed again. "Step-brother. Step-niece."

He closed his eyes again and shook his head, a muscle under his cheek ticking. "Semantics, Ivy. It's wrong because I've watched you grow up, been your uncle, been your family." He opened his eyes and a harsh grunt left him. "Yet still I can't stay away from you."

"But I don't see you as my uncle, not now, Matthew. And I know the way you look at me, how you feel for me, you don't see me as your niece."

He made a deep noise in the back of his throat. "No, I don't see you as my niece, not anymore, Ivy. I see you as a woman, as mine."

"I'm in love with you. I want you, want this."

One of his hands that had held my upper arm moved seductively down to my hand, over my hip, slid along my belly, and stopped right above my pussy. I held my breath.

He leaned in a little bit closer, our mouths so close now. He cupped my pussy, pushing the material of my linen pajamas into my cleft and causing me to rise on my toes.

"Tell me what you want," I asked boldly.

"I want you, Ivy. I want you so fucking bad I ache inside." He took possession of my mouth then, his searing kiss leaving me breathless. His tongue was like silk against mine, and his hand was like fire between my legs.

With his hand between my thighs, pushing the material of my pajama pants up, I couldn't think straight, let alone stand on my own. I gripped his biceps, holding on, letting the pleasure course through me.

"I'm going to have every part of you until you know you're mine," he murmured against my mouth. He leaned back an inch, with his hand still tangled in my hair, and breathed against my mouth. "Damn the consequences, Ivy." He kissed me again, harder this time, and I melted into him, loved that he held me so tightly, so thoroughly.

"Matthew," I moaned against his lips.

"I've tried to fight how I feel for you, tried to stay

away." He pulled back an inch and shook his head. "It's no use. I love you too fucking much to stay away."

"I love you too," I whispered.

He rested his forehead against mine. "How often have you thought about us together, baby?"

God, could I even be honest with him? "So many times," I whispered and leaned up to kiss him, to stroke my tongue along his lips. I felt Matthew's body harden against mine, felt the stiff outline of his dick press against my belly. I was wet, drenched.

I was ready for him.

"Ivy," he groaned, grabbing a chunk of my hair and pulling my head back gently. For a moment all he did was stare down at my face, this look of pure adoration filling his expression. And then Matthew lowered his mouth and started kissing and sucking at my throat, ran his tongue up the length of my neck, and then stopped at the pulse point right below my ear.

I closed my eyes, not able to keep them open as pleasure coursed through me.

Matthew was breathing heavily, the thick length of his erection pressing against my belly, over and over again as he thrust against me. He was so big, so hard for me. I might have been a virgin, but I knew what I wanted, and that was for Matthew to take me irrevocably, to be consumed by me and devour every inch of my body.

I felt drunk from his touch and kisses, and wanted to be so far gone with the feel and taste of Matthew that nothing else mattered, not the repercussions, not the threat that diving into this forbidden love affair could have serious and disastrous consequences.

I didn't care in that moment because I loved Matthew too much.

Matthew started kissing me again, grinding his massive erection against my belly harder, fiercely, like he couldn't get enough, and all I could do was hold on and take it all.

"Matthew," I moaned. "Tell me what you want." I needed to hear him say it.

"All I want is you." He held my face in his hands, tilted my head to the side, and stroked my lips with his tongue. "Only you."

I let my head fall back slightly and closed my eyes once more, loving it when he started stroking my skin with his thumbs, gently, softly, as if he thought I might break. "Then be with me, Matthew."

This growl of need left him and he pulled back to stare down at me for a few seconds, almost like he was struggling with himself about what he should do, if he should stop this before it even got started.

"We deserve this," I whispered.

Despite the chill in the air, I was overheated. My nipples were hard, my panties soaked. I was too

worked up to even try and act like I wouldn't be
pushed over the edge if he blew in my ear.

He said nothing, didn't move even more. I reached
out and flattened my hands on his chest, smoothed
them down, and stopped at the button and fly of his
jeans. My hands started to shake at the thought that I
was about to be with the man I loved, that he would be
moving so hard inside of me. I actually felt lightheaded
from it.

But before I could undo his button, he took hold of
my hands and brought them up to his mouth, kissing
my knuckles.

God, don't stop this.

"Matthew." I breathed out his name, feeling my
hands tremble even harder now. "Don't stop this," I
said out loud this time. I wanted to give him
everything, wanted to be able to pleasure him as much
as he would surely pleasure me. But I knew nothing
about sex, was so inexperienced it was laughable.

He pulled me close and stared into my face. Even
in the darkness I saw his nostrils flare and this
possessive, dangerous look cover his face.

"You're mine." I leaned in close. "No one will ever
know how you feel but me."

I licked my lips and nodded.

Before I knew what was happening, clothes were
tearing and being tossed aside. It was like an animal

was let free inside of Matthew and he let it out, let it be feral.

Matthew had his hands on my hips as he backed me up until the edge of the bed came in contact with the back of my knees. I couldn't breathe, and my knees felt so wobbly, my legs so unsteady.

I slowly lowered myself to the bed and stared up at him, seeing his massive body dominating the space around us, between us. He leaned forward and braced a hand on the bed beside me. We breathed the same air for a second, and then he was kissing me again.

He groaned against my lips, his tongue stroking mine, his actions fierce as he mouth-fucked me. And that's exactly what he was doing, as if he were too unhinged to control himself.

"Your virginity, innocence, is *mine*." He stroked my lips with his tongue, and moved his hand down my chest, teasing the edge of my breast before moving down my belly. He stopped when he got to the top of my pussy, the heat and heavy weight of his hand on my mound wringing a gasp from me.

I stared up at him, my lips parted as I waited for him to touch the most sensitive part of me.

"Your pussy is *mine,* Ivy. No one will know how hot and tight you are, how this virgin pussy feels clenching as you come."

I felt that truth deep in my body, and knew without

a doubt he meant every word. The low throb that had been present between my thighs now became a fierce pounding that demanded to be noticed.

"If only you really knew how I feel for you, that you hold the key to everything that is me." His voice was low and filled with heat. "If you only you knew that I'd take down anyone who thought they could take you from me."

The thick erection he sported had me clenching my thighs together as need overtook me. Sweat bloomed over my body and we hadn't even had sex yet. The force of his breathing brushed across my face, ruffling the tendrils of my hair in a soft caress. His chest rose and fell quick and hard, and the pulse at the base of his throat beat wildly. Was my need just as evident as his?

I lifted my hands and placed them on his hard, defined abdomen, felt the muscles contract under my palm, as if that small touch affected him so much. I moved my hand over the rolling hills of his six-pack and up his chest, his skin warm, firm. And then my palm was right over his heart. The beat was strong and steady.

"Your touch..." He didn't finish what he said as he groaned.

I leaned into him, felt the heat from his body seep into mine, and closed my eyes. I just absorbed it all. It felt good to feel his warmth with nothing between us. It felt incredible to actually be in this situation after thinking about it—wanting it—for so long.

"Look at me," he said softly.

When I opened my eyes and looked into his face, I saw love, lust, and a fierceness reflected back at me. "Be with me," I breathed out. "Be my first, Matthew."

"I'm going to be your only, Ivy."

As much as I wanted to stay in this moment, reality crept in. "This will cause problems. My dad, the town. Everyone." Although I wouldn't stop this for any of that.

"Right now, let's focus on us, not all the shit we'll deal with after the fact." He kissed me softly. "Besides, talking about Stephan right now is a mood killer." He chuckled softly and I did the same.

"Sorry," I said with a smile.

"Never be sorry, least of all to me."

The heavy weight of him against me had everything else fading away.

"I love you," I said softly.

"And I love you." His tone was harsh, gruff. "Now let me finally claim the only woman who has ever had my heart."

15

Matthew

I tried to act like I had my shit together, that I wasn't nervous, but the truth was I was scared as hell. And that was something that didn't happen to me. I didn't fear shit, didn't worry about anything. But with Ivy, I felt like I had the weight of the world on my shoulders.

I stared down at her, took in the sight of her flawless body, felt drunk as I saw the way she stared at me. She looked up as if I had all the answers in the world, as if I'd never let anything happen to her.

And I wouldn't. Never.

My breathing was harsh, erratic. I was hard, stiffer than I'd ever fucking been in my entire life. I knew I shouldn't be touching her, should have more fucking control. But Ivy was my addiction, and I had no intention of breaking the habit.

I stared down at her breasts, the globes a perfect handful, her nipples hard and a dark shade of pink. I reached out and cupped one large breast. My cock jerked and my balls drew up tight. The image of opening her thighs so I could see her sweet, soaked virgin pussy slammed into me.

"How ready are you, baby?"

She didn't answer for a long moment, but I could see the ecstasy written across her face.

"So ready," Ivy finally said. She reached out and curled her nails into my biceps and I got into a better position between her thighs, feeling the hot, wet center of her body, and hissing out from the contact.

"Christ," I said on a guttural groan.

The room was so fucking hot, but my desire for Ivy was hotter.

"No more waiting."

I looked into her eyes and nodded. Yeah, we'd done enough of that. I positioned myself at her entrance, my hand wrapped around the base of my dick, my throat dry and my head fuzzy. I swore time stood still. And then I was pushing into her, breaking through her hymen, burying myself to the hilt inside of her. My balls pressed against her ass, and a gust of air left me.

God.

I didn't move, just stayed still as I smoothed my hand over one of her breasts, cupping the mound, and strumming my thumb over the stiff peak.

Maybe coming into her room, giving in to my desire, had been the wrong fucking move, but I couldn't have stopped myself if a gun had been pointed at my head. So here I was, touching Ivy, my step-brother's daughter, and a woman far too young for me. But I fucking loved her.

I'd do anything for her, even risk my relationship with Stephan for the promise of being with her.

I closed my eyes and just enjoyed the feeling of having her close. Wrapping my arms around her shoulders, I held her tightly and rested my chin on the crown of her head, my cock still buried deep in her body. I felt her pussy walls flutter around my length, but wanted to give her time to get accustomed to me, to my girth.

I wasn't a small man, and my dick was no different. She was tiny compared to me.

Burying my face in her hair, I inhaled deeply. She smelled good, like the beach, warm and bright, fresh with a hint of salt from the sweat that now covered her body.

I needed to be gentle with her, to show Ivy she meant the world to me. I could say that all I wanted, but showing her with my body was an entirely different game altogether. And no matter how wrong people might see being with her, She. Was. Mine.

I pulled back, but instantly leaned down and kissed her soft and slow. With her nails lightly digging into my skin, I was seconds away from letting the beast free and fucking the hell out of her.

Easy.

Slow.

Gentle.

I repeated those words in my head over and over again.

Moving my hand behind her head, I cupped her nape and kept her stationed so I could really kiss her. She moaned and I moved my tongue faster and harder against hers. My body screamed for more, to be rougher, harder, but I fought those urges because right now I needed to show her that I could be gentle when it came to her.

When I pulled back to look down at where we were connected, everything in me froze. Her pussy was stretched wide around my cock, glossy and pink ... all mine. The thatch of trimmed hair that covered the top of her mound had my mouth watering, my cock feeling like it got thicker in her. The sight of her bare pussy lips had my balls drawing up tight, the need to fill her with my cum running strong.

I still had yet to move within her, and instead

smoothed my hands along her inner thighs. For a suspended moment, I did nothing but stare at where we were connected, unable to tear my gaze from the sight. A tightening started at the base of my spine the longer I gazed at her pussy.

"Matthew," she whispered. "Please," she begged.

I needed to make this good for her. "Look at me, Ivy." My voice was hard and serrated. And when she looked at me, we didn't speak, didn't even breathe for long seconds.

I leaned back slightly, bracing one hand on the mattress and slid my other hand up her body and stopping right below one of her breasts. I could feel how fast and hard her heart was beating, how worked up she was.

And then I pulled all the way out, hearing her gasp, but before she could complain, I had my face between her thighs and my mouth on her pussy. I ran my tongue along her slit and up to her clit. She tasted sweet and slightly musky, was soft beneath my lips, and I felt this string in me draw tight before snapping in half. There was the light coppery taste along my tongue, and I knew it was her virgin blood.

That got me hotter than anything else ever had.

I started licking and sucking at her, wrapped my lips around her clit until she was pulling at my hair and moaning for more. Ivy rotated her hips back and forth, thrust her pussy firmly against my mouth, and I hummed in pleasure.

"I want you to come all over my face, baby," I grumbled against her soaked flesh.

The feeling of her tightening her hold in my hair and the hitch in her breath told me she was already so close.

So I sucked on her clit with more fervor, then dragged my tongue down her cleft to gently probe the muscle into her tight little opening.

I felt her explode around my tongue.

Taking my thumb to her clit, I rubbed the bud back and forth, drawing out her pleasure.

"Matthew. I need you back inside of me." Her voice was soft, a pleading note in it. "*Please*," she whispered.

Fuck. She was my undoing.

I caressed her in gentle sweeps of my fingers, mouth, and tongue, until goosebumps formed along her skin. "Every part of you is mine." I moved up her body once more and took her mouth again, and got lost in everything that was Ivy.

"I love you."

I grunted and gripped her chin in a soft hold, waiting until she stared into my eyes. "You were always meant to be mine. I love you, too."

"I'm yours, Matthew."

And then I kissed her hard, possessively. I was about to show her that she was mine.

16

Ivy

This was really happening. No going back now.

His big body rested against mine, pressing me into the mattress and sending an erotic sensation coursing through me.

I felt stretched, full. The discomfort was immense, but having Matthew with me, knowing it was him deep inside of my pussy, made the pain vanish until all I felt was pleasure.

"I want to be gentle with you this first time," Matthew murmured against my throat, and I loved how his stubble scraped along my skin. He was so big and heavy as he pressed his chest down on mine.

Warm, masculine flesh molded into me, making the sweet anticipation of release just a reach away.

"I won't break."

He groaned a second before he moved his hips back and forth, pulling almost all the way out before pushing back inside of me. I didn't want him to see that the sting of pain was there, because that was just a small amount of this experience.

A guttural groan left Matthew, and he jerked his hips forward. "You feel so fucking good. I don't think I'll last."

I rose up slightly and stared down the length of my body. I watched as he thrust his dick in and out of me.

God.

"No more fighting. No more denying," he said as if speaking to himself.

He started a steady thrusting now and I fell back on the bed and breathed out as the sensations moved through me.

"I've wanted you for a long time, Matthew. So long I'm embarrassed to even admit it." I said those words on a moan, not even caring how honest they were.

He pushed up from me, one forearm braced on either side of my head, and looked down at my body. A muscle in his jaw ticked as if he were fighting with himself for control.

"I'm sorry if I'm hurting you." His words were

clipped, his jaw set so tight I heard his teeth gnashing together.

"I'm fine." I held onto his biceps. "I promise." My inner muscles clenched around him on their own and he groaned. I heard him inhale sharply, as if that small act was almost his undoing.

Matthew took one of his hands and placed it between my breasts, as if to keep me steady, keep me in place.

"You're so wet for me, so tight." I watched as his throat worked as he swallowed. "You're so fucking primed for me," he whispered. My nipples tightened as blood rushed to them.

Matthew leaned down and latched his lips onto my neck again, licking and sucking at my skin until it felt pleasurably abraded. He ran his tongue up my throat and a moan left me.

So. Good.

And before I knew what was happening, his mouth was off my neck, his lips suctioned around one of my nipples. Matthew's harsh, guttural groans filled my ears.

"Kiss me," I cried out and he was doing just that instantly.

I swept my tongue along his lips, loving the harsh sound that came from him. The musky, sweet flavor of me was still on him, and I grew wetter from it.

He broke the kiss, his breathing as if he'd run a marathon.

"I can't wait another second."

Thank God.

And when he cupped both sides of my face and kissed me possessively, my pussy clenched around him.

"Christ." He started moving back and forth, faster and harder with each passing second. The broad head of his cock stretched my virgin pussy. When he thrust into me, I moved up an inch on the bed, gasping from the sensations.

Matthew leaned back slightly and watched himself push into me and pull back out. "This means you're mine." He snapped his eyes up to stare at my face. "No one will ever fucking have you but me."

The play of muscles that rippled along his chest and abdomen spoke of his strength, and a gush of moisture slipped from me, further aiding in his penetration. The sounds of wet sex filled my head and I felt my pleasure climb high, my orgasm rising to the surface.

Beads of sweat dotted his brow and slid down his temple. The force it took for him to control himself turned me on even more. His cock slid in and out of me.

"*Christ*, Ivy," Matthew said harshly. He braced

himself on his knees and gripped my inner thighs, pushing my legs impossibly wider as he sank into my body. When he lifted his gaze back to mine, he said hoarsely, "You see how I'm taking you?" I could only nod. "No going back now, baby."

He pulled his cock almost all the way out, and I saw the glossiness from my arousal coating his thick length. He placed his thumb on my clit and moved the bundle of nerves back and forth, over and over, slow and steady.

I exploded for him.

Lights flashed in front of my eyes as my orgasm claimed me. And Matthew didn't relent as he thrust in and out of me, drawing out my climax until my eyes widened and I cried out, unable to stop myself.

I couldn't breathe.

When the world came back into focus, I stared at him. He looked feral, perspiration beaded over his body, his focus trained right on me. His short hair was damp at his temples from the sweat, a sexy look that had my desire climbing once more even though I'd just gotten off hard.

But before I could move, think, even breathe, Matthew was on his back with me straddling his waist, his cock still buried deep in my body.

"Fuck," he groaned. He lifted me easily, forcing his cock to almost slip out. "Christ, baby." He had his gaze trained right on where we were connected. He pushed me down, lifted me up, and did this over and over again until I was dizzy with need all over again.

And all I could do was hold on as he took the reins, took control and fucked me on his dick.

For long moments, he lifted me and pushed me back down on his length, his focus locked on where his cock was, his mouth parted and desire covering his face.

He pressed me all the way down on him.

"Grind that pussy on me, baby."

I did what he said and we both gasped at the sensitivity of it.

He tightened his hold on my waist as I started rocking back and forth, my clit rubbing on him, the ecstasy body-numbing. I was going to come again.

"Come on, Ivy. Give it to me one more time, baby."

And I did just that.

The explosion inside of me had me tossing my head back and crying out. It moved through my entire body, locked up my entire frame, sucked the air from my lungs.

Matthew dug his fingertips into me, and his low, animalistic grunt signaled he'd found his own release.

It felt like a lifetime before reality sank back into me.

I collapsed against his chest, our skin sweaty, our

breathing labored. He wrapped his arms around me instantly and rolled over so that my chest was to his side, my arm slung over his abdomen.

Spasms of pleasures still coursed through me and I closed my eyes and rested my forehead against his damp chest, listening to the sound of his heart beating.

After several minutes of silence, and the feel of Matthew stroking his fingers up and down my side, I pushed myself up and stared down at him. For a second he just stared at me, and then lifted his hand to cup my cheek.

"What is it, baby?" he said softly.

I was silent for a moment. "I'm just worried about how all of this will play out with my dad." I hated that I was thinking about this right after we'd been together. But reality was reality.

"It'll be okay," he said softly. "I'll make sure of it."

I looked over at him. He was staring at the ceiling, his jaw tense as he looked deep in thought. And then he glanced at me.

"I love you," I said softly.

He kissed me on the forehead, and I loved this gentleness in him. He was big and strong, tattooed and had a hard edge to him. But when he was with me, he showed this softer side.

"I love you too." He exhaled slowly and pulled me

in closer. "I'll make sure this works out because I've never loved anyone but you, Ivy, and I never will."

I licked my lips. "This won't end well, Matthew," I whispered against him, keeping him close, knowing very well that if people knew about us, if my father found out, this would end badly.

"Mine, Ivy. You're mine and I don't care about repercussions. I care about you." He kissed the crown of my head and pulled me in closer. "The repercussions are a chance I'm more than willing to take. Because giving you up isn't something I'm going to fucking do."

17

Ivy

The first thing I felt when I woke up was a feeling of being deliciously sore. I was tender between my legs, and when I lightly parted them as I shifted on the bed, I felt the after effects of what Matthew and I had done dried onto my inner thighs.

Although maybe it should have disgusted me, I felt this heat move over me, the feeling of exactly where he'd been, how deep he'd been inside of me, how much he'd stretched me, slamming into me like a thousand tanks.

He'd claimed my virginity.

My eyes were still closed, so when I opened them I blinked a few times, staring at the ceiling, waiting for my vision to clear. I felt a small smile spread across my cheeks. Being with Matthew last night had been everything I'd dreamed of and fantasized about.

He'd been gentle but fierce, consuming but thorough. He'd made sure I felt just as much pleasure, even more, than he did.

I shifted, expecting him to be beside me, but when I saw emptiness, I felt disappointment fill me. The first thing that came to my mind was that he regretted it, had left, and that he'd leave our house because this would just be too difficult.

I knew things would be hard when my father found out, when we told him. There was no getting around that ... there was no going back.

But we were both consenting adults, loved each other, and I wasn't about to give that up.

I wasn't about to give Matthew up.

I pushed myself up on the bed, trying to formulate what I would say to Matthew to convince him that he didn't have to be worried about this blowing up in our faces. But before I could really think of anything, I heard footsteps coming down the hall. A moment later my door was pushed open and Matthew stood there in the entryway, completely bare except for the boxer briefs he wore.

The air left me as I stared at his body. Shoulders so broad he blocked out everything behind him. His waist was narrow, his abdomen defined. He did manual labor day in and day out. He was all male.

He had that cut of muscle on either side of his six-pack, that defined V that had my mouth watering. His legs, thighs specifically, were as thick as tree trunks, toned and powerful, strength pouring off of him in waves.

I was so small, so feminine compared to him.

And his tattoos, ones he did a good job of hiding when he wanted to, covered his arms and chest, even disappearing underneath the elastic of his briefs. His dark hair was disheveled, messy around his head, and I thought about why it was like that.

Because of me. Because of what we'd done.

And then I lowered my gaze back down to his underwear once more, could see the stiff, hard outline of his cock pressing against the material. It hadn't been like that when he'd first come into the room, so that meant me looking at him, staring at him and taking in my fill, had affected him as much as it was affecting me.

"If you keep looking at me like that, Ivy, I won't be able to control myself." His voice had a sharp edge to it, one that moved over my body and had every erogenous zone in me coming alive.

I gripped the sheets beneath me, holding on to them tightly, trying to control my breathing. "Maybe I don't want you to control yourself," I suddenly said softly, nothing but a mere whisper.

I heard him growl low, like this feral animal. He stepped forward—stalked—there was no other way to describe his movements.

Stealthy. Precise.

When he got to the edge of the bed, he braced his hand on the mattress, his focus trained right on me. He reached out and grabbed the sheet that covered me, pulling it slowly off, the material sliding down my body.

My nipples puckered further, and I was so drenched between my legs, I had no doubt a wet spot would form beneath me.

And then he reached out and grabbed my ankles, curling his big hands around the delicate bones, his fingers touching as he slowly pulled me down the mattress. The air left me on a whoosh as I lay on my back now, watching Matthew, knowing what he was about to do.

His eyes were right on me as he pushed my legs apart ... as far as they'd go. My muscles protested from the act, but I obeyed. I did exactly what Matthew wanted because it's what I wanted as well.

I bent my knees and placed my feet flat on the bed. He slid his hands up my calves, pushing me even more open. I was obscenely spread for him, my inner lips parting like a blooming flower.

"I could devour you and it wouldn't be enough, Ivy." He moved in an inch closer and I felt his warm breath move along my pussy. "Because the truth is, I'm starved for you." Matthew looked down between my legs, his eyelids lowering slightly, this half-mast expression now covering his face.

His mouth parted slightly, the air leaving him on a breath. I felt that stream of air move along my exposed lips, causing me to close my eyes and moan harshly.

"Tell me what you want me to do to you, Ivy."

I swore I could feel the vibrations of his voice along every inch of me. My clit throbbed in time with my pulse, and I clenched the sheets even tighter. My neck muscles strained as I rose up slightly and looked at him, keeping my upper body elevated so I could look down the length of my body to see his head between my legs.

I licked my lips, not sure if I could actually say the words, could be so vulgar, to tell him what I wanted him to do to me.

"Tell me," he ordered, commanded in this harsh growl. His hands were clenched tightly on my inner thighs, and all I could think about was how I wanted bruises on my skin, his mark of ownership.

"I want your mouth on me," I whispered, my chest

rising and falling, my stomach hollowing out as my breathing increased.

His hold on me tightened painfully, that agony and pleasure mixing as one. He stared into my eyes for a suspended moment, and then he leaned down and devoured me.

I couldn't hold myself up any longer and fell back on the mattress, closing my eyes and pulling the sheets on either side of me as ecstasy slammed into my body. He licked and sucked on me, sliding his hands closer to my pussy so he could place his thumbs on either side of my lips and pull them apart, really sucking on me then.

Matthew latched his mouth on to my clit, sucking on the bundle of nerves in long pulls, drawing out my pleasure until I was on the precipice of coming, and then slowing down, making me whimper in need.

He flattened his tongue along my pussy hole, dipping it in and pulling it out, pushing it back in and retreating. He did this over and over again, fucking me with that muscle before flattening it again and drawing it up my center and back to my clit.

I was mindless with desire, my lust so potent it was like a living entity inside of me. I was crying, tears falling out of the corners of my eyes as the pleasure continued to soar higher, until I felt like I was drifting above everyone and everything.

He hummed, those vibrations setting me off, having me explode for him.

I cried out as I came, heard his harsh grunt against me, and felt the mattress slightly moving. I knew he was pressing his dick against it, dry humping it.

My legs closed slightly, his head blocking them from touching. I kept him between my thighs, his relentless mouth working me over until I was too sensitive for more. I begged, pleaded, and whimpered for him to stop.

He pulled back and crawled up my body and I forced my eyes open, staring into his, unable to draw enough oxygen into my lungs. And then he kissed me, stroking his tongue along the seam of my lips before plunging inside and making me taste myself on him.

By the time he pulled back I was a withered mess, my body like putty for him, pliable. Every synapse in my brain fired at once.

He moved to the side and pulled me close so we were chest to chest, the semi-stiff outline of his erection pressing against my belly. I reached between us and started stroking his length through the material, and then came across the saturated part of his briefs, right where his cock head was. I sucked in a breath as I realized what had happened.

He gripped my chin with his thumb and forefinger as he stared into my eyes. "You see what you do to me?"

He leaned in and kissed me softly. "You're so fucking hot, so perfect, that you getting off for me had me coming in my fucking underwear like I'm some inexperienced teenager."

He kissed me harder than before and I melted against him. The fact that I could make Matthew lose that much control gave me a wave of power. I felt it move through every single part of my body. This wasn't just a passing fling. I knew that with certainty, felt it.

This was an all-consuming love that would only get stronger with time.

This was a forever kind of thing.

18

Ivy

"Ivy, anyone in there?"

I blinked a few times, the end of my pencil in my mouth as I turned and looked at Georgia. She sat across from me on one of the outside picnic benches on school property. The sun was shining, the weather was perfect, and my mind was on one thing.

Matthew.

I thought about everything we'd done together, how he made me feel. I thought about how he'd taken my virginity, how I was still pleasantly sore between my thighs. That thought had heat rushing to my face and I cleared my throat, setting my pencil down and trying to act like my mind wasn't in the gutter.

The way Georgia lifted a dark brow told me I probably wasn't playing this off as well as I had hoped.

"What are you thinking about, girl?" She wagged her eyebrows.

A gust of wind picked up and blew some of our lunch trash around the table. We scrambled to pick it up, a small reprieve for me from having to attempt to give her part of the truth. I didn't think I could actually be honest with her about it all, couldn't tell her how I felt, that I was in love with my uncle. I trusted her, but I was afraid.

Maybe too afraid.

"Hey, what's wrong?" The genuine concern in Georgia's voice was clear.

I didn't want to be ashamed or afraid. And a part of me wanted to just come clean. This secret weighed heavily on me, was eating me up inside.

I looked into her eyes, knowing that I had to trust her with this, that she'd always had my back. If I couldn't be honest with my best friend, then who could I be honest with?

And so I'd just say it.

"I'm in love, Georgia." Those words spilled from me effortlessly and it felt so good getting them out to someone other than Matthew. Her eyes widened a bit and then she grinned.

"Seriously?" She leaned forward. "Who is it? Does

he go to our school? What's his name? Do I know him?" She fired off the questions one by one and I felt my nerves climb higher.

This was it, the moment I'd finally be honest, truthful with someone. Would it ruin our friendship? Would she think I was disgusting? Or maybe she'd accept it and be there for me.

I could tell she was anxious for my answer, and although I knew this was what I wanted to do, I was also scared shitless. But I took a deep breath then, looked her in the eyes, and just said the biggest secret I'd ever had in my life.

"It's Matthew."

She looked a little confused at first, her brows furrowing as she leaned back. "Matthew? Matthew Hawk from English 101?" I shook my head slowly. "Matthew Jacobson from physics?" I shook my head again. "Please tell me it's not Mr. Richards, our gym teacher."

I wrinkled my nose. "His first name is Matthew? How do you even know that?" I shook my head again. "Never mind." I exhaled. "He doesn't go to school." I licked my lips and started rubbing my hands up and down my thighs.

"He's older?" It was clear she hadn't put two and two together, but then again, who would think someone would be in love with their uncle?

"Yeah, he's older."

"Oh yeah?" Her grin was instantaneous.

"It's Matthew, Georgia. As in my uncle Matthew." I swear the air thickened, as if I were underwater and struggling for breath. Her expression was stoic at first, but I watched it change slowly into shock. Her eyes widened, her mouth opened in a silent O.

The silence stretched between us, and I knew that she probably was speechless. Hell, I knew I would be if the roles were reversed.

"Pretty crazy, huh?" I was still rubbing my palms up and down my thighs, my skin underneath the denim starting to become sore.

I swallowed, this tightness and thickness in my throat almost suffocating. I had this feeling that I had no control of the situation.

Then again, I guess I didn't.

"Well," Georgia said and leaned forward again, her focus on her hands as she stared at them for long moments. "So, this is like a real thing, right?"

"Right."

Georgia started chuckling a little but it sounded awkward. "I don't even know what to say." She sat back again and looked to her left, watching as the girls' soccer team practiced. "Does your dad know?" She glanced back at me and I shook my head. "Yeah, that's probably best, but he'll find out eventually."

I shook my head again.

"Hey," she said and reached out to place her hand on top of mine.

I looked up at her, not realizing that I had glanced down at my lap.

"Everything will be okay."

I loved her optimism, but in this moment, it wasn't reality.

We were silent again for long moments before she spoke again. "Does he love you back?"

I was a little surprised by how she was taking this. Although I hadn't expected any judgment from her, the truth was, I expected the worst. Maybe it was because of the situation and how people would perceive it. I just assumed, pictured, that's how Georgia would react.

I felt a small smile spread across my face as I nodded. "He does."

I watched as a smile formed on Georgia's lips. The way she looked at me ... I knew what she was about to ask and I felt my cheeks heat instantly.

"So have you, you know...?"

With any other person I would've felt a little offended that they'd been so nosy, but this was Georgia. This was the first real thing I'd ever kept from her. She told me when she lost her virginity to Alex Hargrove last year in the back of his pickup truck at a bonfire. She told me when she got her first kiss in ninth grade with Michael Sanders.

We always told each other everything, and the truth was, I wanted to tell somebody about my relationship with Matthew. And that somebody was Georgia.

"Yeah," I said softly and looked around, my face on fire now. I didn't say anything else, and I could see Georgia wanted me to give more details.

"Well?" she said a little impatiently.

"It was..." I stared into her blue eyes and saw the excited look on her face. She rested her head in her hand.

"Incredible? Mind blowing? Everything you've ever thought it would be?" she said dreamily and we both started laughing. "So how long has it been going on? Like, years?"

I shook my head. "No, nothing physical happened until this past week. But I've always loved him."

Georgia sighed dreamily again. "It sounds so forbidden and magical. Like something out of a movie or a book." She straightened and a serious expression covered her face. "Your dad's going to flip his shit when you tell him."

All I could do was nod.

Yeah, when he found out, flipping his shit would be putting it mildly.

19

Ivy

I opened the front door, stepping in and closing it behind me. The only thing I could hear was the sound of the clock in the kitchen ticking down the time. Other than that, there was a heavy silence in the air.

"Hello?" I looked in the living room and found it empty, then made my way into the kitchen. I could hear banging outside, and looked out the picture window by the dining room table to see Matthew working on the gazebo.

My father had started it before he lost his job, a weekend passion project that had been put on hold after he got fired. It looked like Matthew was taking matters into his own hands on that.

I grabbed a glass of water and moved back to the window, leaning against the frame and drinking as I watched Matthew. He was shirtless, had sweat covering his big, tattooed and muscular chest. He had to have been out there for hours to be sweating that much.

God, that was so hot.

I started drinking the water a little bit more until I realized it was completely empty. I focused on Matthew, the way his muscles moved under his skin, the way his biceps flexed when he lifted a piece of wood up ... was also arousing.

I set the glass on the table and breathed out slowly, wiping a drop of water off the corner of my mouth.

The image of his touches, his kisses, the thought of how he looked at me, this hungry expression in his eyes, like an animal hiding right before it pounced on its prey, turned me on until I felt like I'd pass out.

And that's how he looked at me, as if I was his very last meal and he'd consume every single part of me.

I found myself heading out back and right to the gazebo. The fencing around our backyard was high enough the neighbors couldn't see us, but I could hear them talking, could hear the sound of bottles clanking together, could smell the scent of charcoal burning as they fired up the grill.

The sound of Matthew bringing the hammer down was loud, echoing. And the sight of him, with his arms stretched above as he held the piece of wood and hammered a nail in, as his muscles contracted and relaxed, had me wet ... drenched.

My panties were already damp and I felt my nipples tingle. I glanced down to see them pressing against the material of my shirt. I was breathing harder and faster the closer I got to him, the images in my mind so filthy they were making me blush.

I stopped when I was a few feet from him. His back was so wide and broad, his jeans hanging low on his hips, his dark belt keeping them up. He had yet to realize I was right there, so close to him that if I just reached out, I could've dragged my fingers along his perspiration-dampened skin.

His jeans fit him perfectly, not too tight, not too loose. They molded over his big thighs and tapered down to the dark boots he wore. I dragged my gaze back up the length of his spine and craned my neck a little bit so that I'd be able to look at his face when he turned around.

I knew what I wanted to do in that moment, something so dirty, this exhibitionist part of me rising up. And so I took another step closer, and one more until I was just a few inches from him. I lifted my hand then and placed it on the center of his back, his flesh warm from the sun, damp from the hard work he'd been doing.

I felt him stiffen underneath my palm, and slowly he turned to face me. He was so big, as if working out here was increasing his muscle mass by the second. I licked my lips, no words spoken between us as we stared at each other.

And I could see the change in him, the fact he knew I was aroused, the lust moving between us so fiercely I was surprised it didn't knock me down.

I looked behind me at the fence, knowing that although they couldn't see me from their back yard, there was an upstairs window positioned so if somebody looked out it they could see us easily. I looked at the house behind Matthew and saw the same thing.

But that was a risk I was willing to take.

I slipped my hand in his, and then pulled him toward the back of the gazebo, where large pieces of wood were braced against the structure. It gave a little bit of privacy, but not enough that would keep us from prying eyes if it came down to it.

"Ivy," he said in a gruff, guttural voice.

I placed my hands on his chest and gently pushed him back until he was leaning against the slabs of wood. And then I sank to my knees. I looked up at him, seeing that arousal covering his face, watching how his eyelids went half-mast, how his chest was starting to rise and fall a little bit faster.

As I stared into his eyes, I started undoing his belt, and then went to his button and zipper. I pulled the side open and tore my gaze from his to stare down at his dark briefs. His cock was a hard line pressing against the material, so thick and big that my pussy throbbed at the memory of him being buried inside of me.

"God," he groaned.

When I glanced up, I watched as he reached behind with one hand and gripped the edge of the slab of wood, as if to balance himself, to keep himself stable.

I licked my lips, so hungry for him. The fierce growl that came from Matthew had me clenching my thighs together to try and stem off my arousal, but all it did was add pressure to my clit and have me gasping.

And then I reached out and grabbed the edge of his briefs, pulling them down. His cock sprang free, the tip already wet with pre-cum, his heavy breathing urging me on.

His shaft was thick and long, the vein underneath the length visible as blood rushed beneath the surface of the velvety skin. I curled my fingers around the root of his dick, his girth so massive my fingers didn't even touch. My mouth watered, as if it knew what I was about to do would need all the lubrication it could get.

And then I leaned forward, opening my mouth

wide and taking in the head of his cock, forming my lips around the tip and running my tongue along the slit. The whole time I kept my gaze trained right on Matthew. He had his eyes locked right on me, this almost feral expression on his face. His mouth was parted slightly as he breathed harshly.

My head spun and I closed my eyes, hollowing out my lips and taking as much of him into my mouth as I could. He tasted salty but sweet. He tasted like everything I always wanted and finally had.

I really got into it then, opening my throat and taking as much of him as I could, the tip of his cock hitting the back of my throat and making me gag. My eyes watered so much a single tear slipped out of the corner. But I didn't want to stop. I never wanted to. I wanted more, so much more.

I started bobbing my head up and down, humming around his length. What I couldn't reach with my mouth I stroked with my hand, using them in tandem to get him off. I wanted his cum deep in the back of my throat, wanted to swallow it, wanted to take that into me the same way he'd taken my orgasm into him as he ate me out.

My pleasure was breath-stealing, mind-numbing in that moment.

I felt his hands in my hair, his fingers digging at my

scalp. He pulled at the strands until the pain and pleasure mixed as one.

"That's it, Ivy. That's so fucking it." The deep rumble that came from him spurred me on.

I gripped his thighs, curled my nails into his legs, and mouth-fucked him. My gag reflex was strong every time he pushed his hips farther into my mouth, the crest of his cock hitting my throat. And then he'd still, buried all the way in, the oxygen leaving me as he forced me to take every last inch of him.

And I did.

I wanted to make him feel good. Because in turn that made me feel good.

"God, Ivy. Baby."

I opened my eyes and looked up at him, seeing the way his abdomen was clenched, his six-pack in stark relief. His eyes were closed, his head thrown back. He looked like he was in the throes of ecstasy.

"Christ, if you don't stop I'm going to come."

I hummed around his cock and held onto his thighs tighter when he went to pull away. I shook my head, moving my tongue up and down the underside of the length, moaning at the taste of him.

"Fucking hell, Ivy." His hands tightened in my hair and I made a small sound in the back of my throat.

And then he started thrusting his hips back and forth, driving his dick deep in my mouth. My eyes still watered, the need to taste him, to have his seed sliding down the back of my throat too much of a temptation.

I started stroking his cock with my hand, the part I couldn't reach, the need to feel him let go strong. I wanted to be the one to get him off like this, to have him so mindless with his pleasure he couldn't control himself, couldn't stop himself from coming.

"Shit," he grunted out. "Don't stop until I'm shooting my load into your throat, until you're swallowing every last drop." He sounded frenzied, harsh as he demanded those things.

The very knowledge that anybody could see us was an aphrodisiac that made me uncontrollable in my lust.

He slammed his cock as far into my mouth as I could take.

"I'm fucking coming."

I choked on his cockhead but didn't dare pull away when I started to feel the hot, salty thickness of his cum sliding down my throat.

And I swallowed it all, took every last drop until he was the one gently pushing me away, breathing out harshly as he stared down at me.

I stayed on my knees, my hands on my thighs as I looked up at him. I couldn't catch my breath. The flavor of everything that was Matthew filled my mouth.

He looked feral in that moment as he reached out

and ran his thumb along my bottom lip. He lifted the digit up and showed me a drop of his semen on the pad, and promptly pushed his thumb back into my mouth, making me take it. "Lick it clean, baby. I want all of me in you."

For long moments, I just sat on the ground at his feet, looking up at him, his finger in my mouth, my tongue running over the digit.

"I love you," he said softly, but the determination in his voice, the sincerity that I heard, had a little sound escaping me.

He lulled his thumb from my mouth and tucked himself back in his jeans, zipped up his pants and fixed his belt. He helped me off the ground and pulled me in, just holding me, his hand on the back of my head as it rested over his heart.

"I love you too," I replied softly, closing my eyes and wishing that this moment would last forever, that reality wouldn't intrude.

He gave me a kiss on the crown of my head before pulling back. But he didn't let me go just yet. He cupped my chin with his thumb and forefinger, tipped my head back, and brought his mouth down on mine, kissing me softly, soundly. It was during that kiss that I heard the back sliding glass door open.

We broke away at the same time, my heart instantly racing.

"Ivy? Matthew?" The sound of my father's voice had panic rising in me.

The last thing I needed was to have him see us in this situation, to find out this way.

We broke away and I looked around in a panic but finally saw a hammer lying on the ground. I grabbed it and held it up to show Matthew. He lifted a dark brown eyebrow and smirked.

"What do you plan on doing with that thing?"

I shrugged. "Working on the gazebo," I said in a hushed whisper.

"Ivy? Matthew?" My father hollered out again and I walked to the other side of the gazebo, where he couldn't quite see me. And then I started hammering. I heard Matthew chuckling as he walked around the other side.

"Over here, Stephan. Ivy and I are just working on the gazebo."

I could see Matthew through an opening in the structure and he winked.

I heard my father and Matthew talking and then finally moved around to the other side, hammer still in hand. They stopped their conversation and glanced at me, my father looking at the hammer I held, surprise on his face. It's not like I did this kind of thing so it probably seemed pretty unusual.

"Hey," I said nervously, my voice shaky. "You're

home." He walked up to me and gave me a hug. I felt guilty, knowing I'd just been on my knees sucking Matthew's dick.

"Yeah, I wanted to surprise you guys." He looked between us and then stared at the gazebo. "You've been helping Matthew with this thing?"

I felt my face heat and nodded.

"It's coming along," he said happily, proudly. "Thanks for working on it," he said to Matthew and glanced at me. "I didn't know you were into this kind of thing."

"Me either." I heard Matthew chuckle at that.

"I wanted to start working on it again, but with the whole job situation, I haven't really had time or the mindset to mess with it."

"No worries," Matthew said and shoved his hands in the front pockets of his jeans. "It keeps me busy." He glanced over at me, and I could see the sheepish look on his face.

My father and Matthew talked for a few more minutes, and as I was about to head back inside, I heard my father clear his throat. "Ivy, I was wondering how you'd feel about me making us dinner tonight." I felt my brows knit in confusion.

Why would he need to ask me how I felt about him cooking tonight? "I'm fine with that." He cleared his throat and lifted his hand to rub it over the back of his neck. He was nervous.

"I was going to invite Cora over." He looked up at me, having glanced away just a moment ago.

I felt a genuine smile spread across my face. "I'd like that. I think it's time we all met." I saw the relief on my father's face as he nodded and grinned back at me.

As I glanced at Matthew, I knew that I was done waiting. We needed to tell my dad about us. It was time.

20

Ivy

I heard the doorbell ring and glanced over at Matthew, seeing his eyes widen in faux surprise. I couldn't help but laugh. The fact that in just a matter of seconds I was about to meet my father's girlfriend—his much younger girlfriend—left me a little on edge.

I was nervous, not so much of her age, but just the fact that he was actually seeing someone. In all the years since my mother had passed, I'd never seen him with another woman. So my anxiety was on those grounds, if I'd inadvertently feel some kind of resentment because she was "replacing" my mother.

Matthew and I stood and walked toward the foyer. I heard my father open the front door, could hear the lower rumble of his deep voice followed by the soft feminine pitch of hers. I felt Matthew's big hand land in the center of my back. He moved his palm up and down along my spine, and I knew he was trying to comfort me, to let me know everything would be okay without saying the words.

"Ivy," my father said from the foyer, loud enough for me to hear.

I looked up at Matthew and he gave me a smile. He leaned down and kissed me on the forehead and I closed my eyes and breathed out slowly. Although my father couldn't see us, I knew if he had noticed it probably would've seemed less intimate than it really was.

"You got this," Matthew said against my head and I nodded.

I broke away from him just as my father stepped around the corner. And then a second later I saw her.

She was beautiful, with bobbed blonde hair, side-swept bangs, and the biggest blue eyes I'd ever seen.

"Ivy, Matthew, this is Cora Lourdes."

Cora smiled, her rosy red lips having a light glossy sheen to them.

"Hi," she said in a melodic voice.

Matthew was the first to respond, holding out his hand and giving a gruff, "Hey, I'm Stephan's brother."

And then the room seemed to go quiet as I felt

everyone's gaze on me. It was as if they were waiting for me to give the okay, or maybe to freak out.

I saw the way he placed his hand on the small of her back, bringing her in close to his side. I didn't miss the way she tipped her head back and looked into his face, the genuine smile and look of adoration in her expression.

"It's really nice to meet you, Cora," I finally said and held my hand out. She slipped her palm against mine. Then it was as if that tension in the room dissipated, as if it was gone as soon as it had arrived.

———

WE'D JUST FINISHED EATING and the atmosphere in the dining room was easy, comfortable. We got to know Cora a little better, found out she was working toward completing her bachelors in nursing, and after that getting her masters as a nurse practitioner. She was driven and smart, funny and articulate.

I definitely could see why my father had been so drawn to her.

And the truth was, I hadn't even thought about their age gap once. Maybe it was because of the age difference between Matthew and me, but I could truly see they cared about each other, and that outweighed anything else.

Matthew sat beside me and I felt his hand on my thigh. He gave me a reassuring squeeze. I looked over at him, the sound of my father and Cora talking drowning out everything else.

They were in their own little world, and I was in mine. My father and Cora probably didn't even notice the little looks Matthew and I gave each other during dinner. And that was probably for the best.

We were still trying to decide how we were going to tell him about our relationship. Because every time I thought it was a good time, it just didn't feel right, or I got too scared about how it would all go down.

Soon though, much sooner rather than later because I hated hiding this from him and being with Matthew behind his back. I wanted to be honest with my father, to show him how much I loved Matthew and he me. I wanted to show him, tell him, that it wasn't wrong.

That it was right.

"You want to go out and get a drink?" I heard my father say to Cora and I glanced over at them, saw the way he had his chair pushed right up next to hers, had his arm wrapped around her shoulders.

She smiled and nodded, and when she glanced over at me and saw that I watched her, I saw her cheeks turn pink. I gave her a smile. I liked her. Not just because she seemed genuine and sweet, but because she loved my father and made him happy. And how could that make me mad?

"You're okay with us heading out?"

I was surprised my father seemed to be looking for my approval on it. But then again, this was probably a little strange for him as well. He hadn't been in a relationship in years, not any that I knew about anyway.

Matthew's hand was still on my thigh, but there was nothing sexual about it. It was a reassuring touch.

I shrugged. "I'm absolutely fine with it all," I said honestly. My father exhaled and I could see that he'd been holding his breath, probably so stressed and worried about tonight that he'd been beside himself.

I couldn't blame him. It was one of the reasons I hadn't told him about Matthew yet. Although my situation was a lot different than my father's, I hoped that when the truth came to light, he would be understanding and accepting, or at least could work up to that.

I knew at first all hell would probably break loose.

An hour had passed, my father and Cora had gone, and Matthew and I had cleaned up. The two of us now sat on the couch with the TV volume almost too low to hear anything, and my body pressed against his. It was dangerous being this close under my father's roof, what with him able to come home at any moment, but he'd probably be out for a couple of hours, and I wanted this small moment where Matthew and I could just be ... us.

He had his arm around my shoulder, his fingers lightly tracing my skin. I felt drowsy, could fall asleep this way. I wanted to.

As if he read my mind, or I'd spoken those words aloud, he shifted slightly so he could grab the blanket off the back of the couch and put it over my legs and waist. I smiled but he couldn't see me. I snuggled in closer to him and closed my eyes.

The feeling of Matthew's chest steadily rising and falling as he breathed lulled me to sleep.

And the one thing that kept playing through my mind was how I wished we could stay like this forever, where there was no judgment, no worries.

Where it was just two people living their lives.

21

Matthew

I should have let her study, concentrate on her work, but all I could do was stare at her. For the last week since Stephan had been home, trying to keep my distance from Ivy, trying not to be a bastard and have her in every way imaginable while my brother was home, was harder than fucking hell.

She was my weakness, the only thing I'd ever wanted fully, selfishly. I couldn't count how many times I'd wanted to just pull my brother to the side and come clean, to be honest. Lying to him, hiding this, felt—was —wrong on every level.

My arousal took a back seat as a seriousness filled me.

"We need to tell him," I said and she glanced up.

"I know," Ivy said right away and leaned back, pushing her book in front of her and exhaling. "We've needed to tell him for the past week."

I lifted a hand and rubbed it over my jaw. "Tonight," I said and she nodded. I was done hiding this, going behind his back. I wanted Stephan to know Ivy was mine and I wouldn't step back, no matter what. I expected fallout, but hell, anything worth fighting for didn't come easy.

I stared out at the gazebo, thought about when Ivy had come out there ... at the memory of what she'd done as she sunk to her knees in front of me.

And just like that I was hard.

I looked over at her, could see she was staring at the gazebo as well, and this low growl left me at the knowledge that she was thinking about that moment too.

"I'm always so fucking hungry for you." I leaned forward. "So. Fucking. Hungry."

She let out a little gasp and I found all self-control leaving me.

The only thing I wanted, saw, felt, in that moment was Ivy. I wanted her, wanted to claim her, put my mark on her ... in that very moment.

I was out of my chair and had her in my arms seconds later. With my hand on her nape, I moved us backward until the wall stopped our retreat.

Mine.

I dipped my gaze down to her lips and didn't stop myself from taking her mouth in a deep, penetrating kiss, fucking her like I had between her legs with my mouth and cock.

I groaned, not stopping myself even though I should have.

"Matthew," she moaned against my mouth and I slammed my hands on the wall beside her head, pressing my hard cock into her belly. A hoarse groan left me when she stroked her tongue with mine.

"I need you," she whispered against my lips.

Fuck, I needed her too.

I slid my hands down the wall, touched her shoulders, stroked her arms, and took hold of her hands. I lifted her arms up, resting the back of her hands on the wall and moving my thumbs over to the pulse points at her wrists. They beat frantically.

My cock throbbed behind my jeans. I wanted to be buried deep inside of her.

She moaned, let her head fall back against the wall, and I started kissing her throat. I thrust against her belly again, and wanted to just pull her pants down, tear her panties aside, get my dick out, and push right into her wet little body.

I didn't stop myself from groaning against her neck. "Fuck, baby girl."

"Take me. Right here. Right now."

I reached between our bodies, starting to unbutton my pants. I'd fuck her right here, right now, just like she wanted. I'd fuck her against the wall until she came all over my cock.

But the sound of the front door opening and closing had me lifting my head from the crook of her neck and looking over my shoulder.

"Ivy? Matthew?" Stephan called out. "I have good news." I could hear him setting his things down in the foyer, but it was like everything was in slow motion. "I got a full-time job offer."

Before I could move or put Ivy back on her feet, I watched as Stephan walked in.

He stopped in his tracks as he looked at us, as he stared at me holding his daughter up against the wall. For several seconds, the three of us didn't speak, didn't move, hell, didn't even fucking breathe. We were all frozen in place.

I should have put Ivy down, but I couldn't move. Stephan stared between us, his expression showing he didn't know what the fuck was going on.

"Matthew," she whispered softly.

I looked at her, saw she was scared as hell, and finally I set her down.

"Dad," Ivy said softly, her voice telling how this affected her.

I wanted to protect her, to shield her from all of this, from the downfall that was surely about to happen.

————

Stephan

There was no fucking way I was seeing what was right in front of me. No fucking way Matthew had my little girl pressed up against the wall, his dick hard, what they were about to do really damn clear.

Matthew had set Ivy on the ground, but I didn't miss how he pushed her behind him, as if to protect her from *me*.

I saw red, was fucking livid. I couldn't have stopped myself if I tried.

I started throwing fists left and right, but Matthew just took it. He didn't fight back, didn't try and stop me.

The sound of Ivy's voice couldn't pierce the thickness of my anger. "How long have you been fucking my daughter behind my back, Matthew?" I cursed those words out. I swung out again, over and over again.

Still, Matthew took everything I gave.

Matthew grunted when I connected my fist with

his mouth. I saw the way his lip split, watched as the blood welled up and then dripped down his chin.

"So instead of waiting for me to come back home to talk to me about all of this, you claiming my daughter like she's yours was the right move?" I didn't hold off the growl that left me. "She's my *nineteen*-year-old daughter, Matthew." I started to pace, my emotions wild and turbulent, violent.

I didn't stop the low sound that came from me. All I fucking felt was rage.

I charged forward again and tackled Matthew to the ground. We crashed against the wall, a few pictures fell to the ground, glass shattering and the sound of Ivy crying out ringing in my head.

I glanced over at Ivy between hits, seeing that she had her hands covering her mouth as she looked on in horror. We should have stopped fighting for her sake, but all I felt was this deep burning rage filling me.

And as I slammed my hand into Matthew's face again, my brother refused to fight, to hit me back.

"I won't fight you, Stephan," Matthew roared out right before I threw my fist into his gut.

That just pissed me off even more. I slammed my fist into any available inch of Matthew I could reach. All I heard was the sound of my heart pounding in my ears. All I felt was the rush of blood moving through my veins.

Matthew pushed me away. "Stephan. Stop. I'm not going to fucking fight you."

"Come on, *brother*. Fucking hit me back. Fight me."

I heard Ivy screaming out. A moment later, amidst the hitting and grunting, the sound of roars that came from me, I sensed Ivy coming closer.

The sound of crunching filled my head and I felt her touch my shoulder. She tried to pull me back, but right now there was nothing short of a SWAT team pulling me off of Matthew.

She tugged harder, screamed out my name to get my attention, but the force of our fighting had her letting go. She cried out in pain and I instantly stopped.

"Fucking hell, Stephan," Matthew roared out and pushed me away as he went over to Ivy.

I stood there and watched as he tended to her, making sure she was okay. Blood covered his face, and I could see he was in pain, but he focused solely on Ivy.

Matthew straightened when it was clear Ivy was fine, pulled her behind him, and narrowed his eyes at me.

"Stephan, I'm not fucking giving her up."

I was shaking my head. No way I was hearing this bullshit. Blood marred Matthew's face, his lips busted open, a cut above one of his eyes.

"Out of all of the women in the world you could

have been with, Matthew, you go after my daughter, your fucking niece?"

"Step-niece," Ivy said instantly. "We aren't related. It's not wrong."

I shook my head as I looked at her. "He's been part of your life, Ivy. He's family."

She looked at Matthew again. "I love him, Dad," she whispered.

I couldn't speak, didn't know what to say.

"I tried to stay away," Matthew said, the sorrow in his voice clear.

"We didn't want you finding out this way."

"Yeah, that's pretty fucking clear," I said, hearing how pissed off I sounded. I started pacing the floor, running my hand over the back of my head and breathing in and out.

"We were going to tell you," Matthew said and took a step forward.

"Oh, you were?" I said sarcastically. "When? After you defiled her against my wall? After you betrayed me over and over again?"

Matthew growled out, "Be pissed at me. Hate me, fucking kick my ass, Stephan, but don't ever fucking talk about Ivy that way." There was this warning tone in his voice. "I won't fight you over this because I admit being with her behind your back was wrong, but I *will* fucking kick your ass if you disrespect her."

My chest was rising and falling fast, and I clenched and unclenched my hands at my sides. As I stared at both of them, a part of me wanted to be happy for my daughter, that she was loved and was in love. But another part, a bigger one, couldn't get past the fact this was my brother in a relationship with my daughter. Blood related or not, we were all family.

"Dad," she said softly and moved closer to me. "This wasn't something we planned. It just happened."

I hated that she was upset and that I had made it worse.

"You can't help who you love," she said and I knew she was talking about my relationship with Cora.

I couldn't look at her, not after all of this, not with how I looked: upset, disappointed, shocked … sad.

What the hell had happened? What a fucking shit storm this had turned out to be.

22

Matthew

I knew being with Ivy would ruin things, knew Stephan would be upset, but fuck, actually living through it, seeing the rage on his face, feeling the punches he threw ... really drilled it all home.

Stephan had headed out back, the door slamming shut, the silence deafening.

"I should go talk with him," Ivy said and I turned to face her.

"No, baby. Let me handle it." I walked up to her and cupped her cheeks, smoothed my thumbs along her cheeks. "Let me see if this is salvageable."

I gave her one more kiss before turning and heading out back. I closed the door behind me and stared at Stephan. He leaned against the banister of the deck, his hands clasped in front of him.

There was the faint smell of exhaust in the air from the few cars that had driven by, and the sound of kids playing in the distance. A truck blasting rap music drove by the house, drowning out my thoughts and how I hoped this would all go.

Stephan looked over his shoulder at me, and I saw the cigarette hanging from his lips.

"I thought you quit years ago," I asked and stepped onto the deck.

He pulled the cigarette out of his mouth and I saw it wasn't even lit.

"I did, but I keep one in case the world ends or some shit."

I snorted and leaned against the railing a few feet away. "The end of the world? Seriously, man?"

He didn't crack a smile as he stared straight ahead, the unlit cigarette hanging between his fingers. "It feels like the fucking end of the world."

Stephan looked at me again. "You look like shit."

My face throbbed at the mention of the fight, but I welcomed the pain. I deserved it.

For a few moments, the only sound was all the noise pollution surrounding us. And then Stephan straightened and crossed his arms over his chest.

"I fucked up by not telling you, Stephan."

He stayed silent.

"I love you. You're my brother, my family, but I won't let her go. I can't. I love her enough to deal with any repercussion being together causes."

Stephan exhaled, sounding defeated.

"I've never loved anyone the way I love her, Stephan. She's it for me."

"It's wrong," my brother said again, as if he wanted to say it over and over again. I couldn't blame him.

"It doesn't feel wrong."

Stephan closed his eyes and shook his head.

The silence stretched out between us for a few seconds. There was a hell of a lot I wanted to talk about, but didn't know what to say that hadn't already been spoken.

And still Stephan remained silent.

"It was wrong to do it behind your back, but that's the only thing I'm apologizing for. Because what I feel for Ivy is real."

Stephan stared at me. "I know you care about her, but see it from my point of view."

I did.

"I know you need time to process all of this, to understand it even, and I can give you that time." I felt my body grow harder. "But hear me on this, Stephan. You can beat my ass and I won't fight back, but I won't let her go."

I'd said all I could. It was up to Stephan to know that it was the truth.

"I don't know whether I can be okay with this." He ran a hand over the back of his head. "She's my daughter, Matthew. You're my—"

"I know," I said softly. "Believe me. I beat myself up over it for so long it was eating away at me."

"A part of me wants to pack her up and get her the fuck out of here. I want to protect her."

"So do I," I said with determination in my voice.

We stared at each other for long moments.

"I love her, Stephan. I'll take care of her with my life."

"People won't understand," he said instantly.

I shook my head. "They don't have to. No one has to understand because it's no one else's business. The only opinion we care about is yours, Stephan. That's all that matters."

23

Ivy

I found my father working on his car in the garage, the sound of classic rock pumping through an old, outdated radio he had sitting on his workbench. The banging of a tool hitting the cement seemed overly loud, but not as loud as my heart racing.

It had been several days since he'd found out about Matthew and me, and although we hadn't ignored each other, I definitely felt the tension between us.

I took another step into the garage, seeing his big body hunched under the hood of his car. He cursed and pulled back, shaking his hand and looking down at it. And then he glanced over at me, a momentary expression of surprise covering his face before he masked it.

"Hey," I said softly and smiled.

"Hey," he said roughly and went over to his workbench to grab another tool.

More silence descended and I felt the awkwardness grow. I twisted my hands in front of me, looking down at them, hating that there was this wall between us. I couldn't blame him, but I wished he would talk to me about it.

I heard him clear his throat and I glanced up, seeing him lean against his workbench, his arms crossed over his chest and his focus on me.

"We should probably talk about this, right?" His voice was pitched low, but it was gentle, maybe even understanding.

I nodded, not trusting my voice in that moment. But silence wouldn't solve anything. "Although I don't know where to start," I finally said.

"I'm not sure either, sweetheart," he said softly. "But I spoke with Matthew. He pretty much told me everything." He looked down at his boots and exhaled again. "It's hard to grasp, I won't lie. But at the end of the day, I just want you to be happy." He looked up at me again and I swallowed roughly. "I just want to know that you're taken care of, that you succeed in life, and that you're loved. That's all I've ever wanted."

God, I was going to cry if this kept up.

"Your happiness has been the only thing that I've ever been concerned about, Ivy. It's why I kept my relationship with Cora from you for longer than I should have. That's why I didn't tell you about me losing my job right away." He shook his head slowly and stared me in the eyes. "Because I figured that would be a blow to your happiness, and I didn't want that."

"I am happy. I'm really happy, Dad. And I'm happy for you." He gave me another smile but it was sad.

"You've just been through a lot. Losing your mother, dealing with your old man dating a woman close to your age, worrying about if we'd lose the house or not." He cleared his throat as if he were uncomfortable talking about this. "I felt a lot of shame and guilt."

I was the one shaking my head now. "You never have to feel those things. I'm happy for you and Cora. I'm glad you found a job. I had no doubt that things would work out."

"Yeah, and it's partly thanks to Matthew. He stepped up. Manned up. He helped me when I was down and had no one to turn to. He didn't give me shit for being with Cora, didn't judge me for the age gap. But I guess I couldn't see past everything ... him being my step-brother, the age difference between the two of you." He sighed again. "Him being with my daughter. I just couldn't see past any of it."

I didn't know what to say, didn't know how to smooth things out, and although I could see my father had come to terms with it all, I wanted us to be back to where we had been before.

So I stepped up to him, just a foot from him now, and wrapped my arms around his waist to give him a hug. In that moment, I felt like a little girl, looking up at my father because he held the world in his hands.

He wrapped his arms around me and just held me, and I closed my eyes and let everything else drift away.

"I'm glad you're happy," he whispered against my hair and I smiled.

"I'm glad we're both happy."

He kissed the crown of my head again. "It won't be easy though," he said again. "People won't be kind."

I pulled back and looked up at him. "I know." He pushed some of my hair away from my cheek. "But you're strong, like your mother was. She didn't take crap from anyone. And if they give you shit, you give them shit right back." I chuckled. "You love him and he loves you, and that's all a father can want for his daughter."

He pulled me in for another hug and it was nice, comforting, and it gave me hope that everything would be fine.

————

I LOOKED up to see my dad by the grill, a roll of hotdogs placed on the grate, the sound and scent of sizzling meat filling the air.

Cora was standing by Georgia, and Charlie was beside her. It was just a little get together, one my father had organized, which surprised the hell out of me.

He'd never been one for gatherings, but there were a lot of things I'd noticed changing in him and his newfound happiness.

Over the last few weeks, Cora had been a steady constant in our lives, and I couldn't deny that I loved seeing her with my father. It was clear he made her happy and she him. He seemed younger, more full of life when she was here.

I felt the heavy weight of hands gently land on my shoulders, giving them a squeeze. I tipped my head back to see Matthew standing there, looking down at me with a smile on his face. He leaned down and kissed the top of my head and I closed my eyes, loving that we could show this small affection in front of everybody and not have to feel shame about it or worry about judgment.

I wished he'd really kiss me, place his lips on mine, a kiss that would have my toes curling. But he didn't like showing affection in front of my father, even if he was okay with our relationship.

And I understood Matthew's hesitancy.

He sat down beside me and slipped his hand in mine, bringing our conjoined hands to rest on his lap. We said nothing as we just watched the four other people at the bbq.

"I haven't seen Stephan this happy since he was with your mom," Matthew finally said softly and I looked over at him.

Although I was very young when my mother passed away, I did have some memories of her and my father together. The way she'd smile at him, the fact he always wanted to hold her hand when we were out in public. But when she'd passed away, I saw a part of my father die right along with her. Then Cora came along, and she breathed new life into him, made him seem like a younger man. And I loved it. I loved her for that.

"Is this weird?" Matthew asked and I looked at him beside me.

I smiled and shook my head. "Honestly, it feels right." It felt like this was how it always should have been. "What do you think?" I asked and looked over at Matthew.

He was silent for a second, bringing his beer bottle up and taking a long drink as he watched everyone. When he set it down there was a small smile on his lips. "Yeah, it really does feel like this is how it should've always been."

My dad brought the plate of steak and hotdogs, chicken and ribs to the table. Everyone sat around, passing the side dishes, laughing, talking, the atmosphere just overall comfortable.

Charlie was enamored with Georgia, Cora was smiling at my father, and Matthew sat right beside me as close as he could get, his arm slung around the back of my chair, his body heat seeping into me.

This was perfection, every little moment, every second of life not being wasted. I'd never known what truly being happy was, but as I looked at Matthew, I knew this was what life was all about.

EPILOGUE

Ivy

Matthew pulled up to the university and I felt like it was the first day of high school. I was scared and nervous, not sure that I'd actually succeed in this.

"Hey," he said softly and placed his hand on my thigh. "You're going to do fantastic."

I glanced at him and he was smiling. I leaned over and placed my lips on his.

Over the summer things hadn't really changed very much. Although Matthew still lived with my father, he was looking for a place of his own now that my dad had a full-time job. Not to mention Cora was over constantly and I knew they wanted their private time. Even though I was starting college, I was driving back and forth, and so now more than ever I felt like I was intruding on them even though my dad assured me I wasn't.

They didn't know I'd overheard them talking about Cora moving in. So I really needed to decide what I was going to do, because commuting while Cora was thinking about moving in was not something I wanted to do. I should've gotten a dorm.

"Cora's thinking about moving in." Matthew didn't say anything, but I could tell by his expression he already knew. "You knew?"

"I overheard your dad talking on the phone with her one day. I didn't say anything because I figured it wasn't my place."

"Yeah, I overheard them too. They haven't talked to me about it yet, so they're either up in the air with the decision, or afraid to tell me." I exhaled. "I told my dad and Cora I'm happy for them, and I assumed she was going to move in eventually. I just wish you would feel comfortable enough to let me know these things."

He drew me into him for a kiss.

"I should've just gotten a dorm," I said against his mouth and gave him one more lingering kiss before pulling away and looking back at the university.

"Or, how about you can just move in with me?"

I was taken aback and leaned away, looking him in the eyes. "Move in with you?"

He shrugged his broad shoulders and gave me a half smirk.

"Would it be the worst thing?"

I smiled and shook my head.

"At least then your dad and Cora can have a place of their own and you don't have to actually walk in on them doing it."

I wrinkled my nose. "Kind of like what he did with us ... almost?" Now it was his turn to grimace.

"Let's not talk about that."

I started laughing and placed my hand on his thigh. He put his on top of mine and gave it a light squeeze.

"I was being serious, Ivy. Move in with me. I can take you to school every day, make sure you get there safely, pick you up, and bring you back to our place and fuck you."

Our place.

I felt my face heat from his obscene comment and promptly felt arousal rise up.

"We can pick out a place together, make it ours."

God, that sounded so perfect.

I looked around the lot where we were parked and saw only a couple of cars on the far end. We were kind of isolated, with trees behind us and right outside the driver side.

Maybe I should have taken things a little more

seriously, prepared myself for the first day of classes. But instead, I found myself crawling over the seat and gear stick, straddling Matthew's waist and placing my hands on his chest, gently pushing him back.

"Ivy?" he asked but promptly groaned when I ground myself on him.

He growled low and placed one hand on the small of my back, his other one gripping my waist. He pushed me down gently and I felt the stiff outline of his erection digging between my legs.

"Fuck, baby." He was breathing heavily.

"This is crazy, but feels so good." I moaned those words out.

He cupped the back of my head, his fingers tangling in my hair. Matthew dragged his tongue over the seam of my lips. I parted them in a gasp, grinding myself against his erection, wanting nothing more than to reach between us, unzip his pants, pull his dick out, and shove it deep in my body.

But I wasn't a fiend, even if I felt like one with Matthew.

I pulled back and saw the drowsy, aroused expression on his face. "Let's shelve this for tonight?" I asked softly.

He groaned and leaned forward to try and kiss me again, but I shook my head, knowing if I didn't things would get heated and I wouldn't be able to stop. I'd want him too badly.

"Tonight?" I asked again and he grunted in clear frustration and rested his head back on the seat.

"Tonight, I guess." He grinned, flashing straight white teeth. "So does that mean you're moving in with me?"

I tried to feign seriousness, but when he pulled me closer so my chest was pressed to his, I squealed in delight. "I mean, it would solve a lot of my problems." He started tickling my sides.

"Oh yeah, that's why you'd want to move in."

The act of me shifting and squirming on top of him caused my pussy to rub against the outline of his thick cock. All amusement faded and we both let out a gasp.

"You know I love you. Living with you will just bring everything full circle," I whispered.

"You moving in with me is what I want, what I've wanted for a while now. I just didn't want to seem like I was rushing you."

I shook my head and placed my hands on either side of his face, the scruff underneath my palms making me feel so very feminine. "That's what I want too," I said honestly.

The silence stretched between us for long moments.

"It doesn't matter where you went to school, Ivy."

He slipped his hand to my nape, looking down at my lips. "It doesn't matter because wherever you would've gone, I would've followed."

I didn't think I could fall in love with Matthew any more than I already was, but every day he surprised me.

The End

PROFESSOR

USA TODAY BESTSELLING AUTHOR
JENIKA SNOW

PROFESSOR

By Jenika Snow

www.JenikaSnow.com

Jenika_Snow@Yahoo.com

Copyright © March 2019 by Jenika Snow

First E-book Publication: March 2019

Photographer: Wander Pedro Aguair

Cover model: Andrew Biernat

Cover photo provided by: Wander Book Club

Editor: Kasi Alexander

Line editor: Lea Ann Schafer

Proofreader: Read by Rose

Cover created by: Mayhem Cover Creations

The things I knew about her, the way I watched. It was all to protect her, all to know her.

She liked her tea with milk and sugar, extra sweet just like I knew her lips would be if I were to kiss her.

I was desperate for her.

She chewed on her pencil when she was concentrating, her little tongue coming out and moving along her bottom lip.

I was hungry for her.

She played with the ends of her hair when she was nervous, her fingers delicate, long, like she played piano, her nails painted pink.

The things I thought about her doing with those tiny hands.

And she bit her bottom lip when she was worried, those straight white teeth sinking into the red flesh, like an apple being broken into, the crack of it consuming.

I didn't deny I wanted her. I didn't even try and hide it.

Innocent. That's what she was.

I stalked her, knew her every like and dislike ... obsessed over her.

I wanted her like I'd never wanted anything in my life. And I told myself that watching her, following her, was to keep her safe. To keep her mine.

I was her professor. She was my student. It was wrong to need her the way I did. But she consumed me, like I was gasping to breathe and she was oxygen.

I was a selfish bastard, and when it came to Grace, I wanted her all to myself.

1

Professor Goode

It's said that an obsession is an idea or thought that continually preoccupies or intrudes on a person's mind.

But I say it's more than that, more than a definition, a string of words thrown together. Nothing can accurately describe how I feel, what I feel, the lengths I'd go to, to get what I wanted, who I wanted.

They'd say I was obsessed.

I called it love.

I remember the first day I saw her, how she looked, how I instantly felt. It had been hot outside, slightly humid, unusual for the time of the year. She'd had a sheen of perspiration on her temple, and I'd wanted to run my tongue along it, gather it up so I'd take a part of her into me.

I remember the first time I saw her like it was yesterday.

The first day she'd put her spell on me.

The first day I'd fallen in love with her.

The first day I'd become obsessed.

I'd known from that moment on, no other would have her. She was mine, and I'd make her see that.

She'd walked into the classroom in this white sundress, these little black flowers splattered across it like spilled ink. Her dark hair had been piled high on her head almost haphazardly, like she'd been running late and hadn't known what to do with it.

Strands had fallen down as if she'd been running, the tie in her hair unable to keep the locks in place. Her cheeks had been pink, and I'd wondered if they'd be that color when she felt pleasure.

Her breathing had been rapid, her chest rising and falling, her breasts pressed against the bodice of her dress, her nipples hard as they'd poked against the thin material.

She'd apologized to everyone she'd walked by as she made her way to her seat, and I followed her the entire time, tracked her with my gaze, unable to pull my focus off her.

She screamed innocence and vulnerability, with

her delicate beauty that had made the very male part of me rise up. Never had I felt such an instant attraction, such a bone-deep arousal.

And it was in that very moment that I knew without a shadow of a doubt I had to have her.

She was my student.

I was her professor.

It was against the rules.

But that made no difference to me. I was born to break the rules for her. I'd realized that as soon as I saw her, as soon as she'd sat in my class. Even now I thought about the way she'd crossed her legs, her dress rising up, exposing even more of her alabaster skin, as if she rarely went out in the sun.

Everything from her pink painted toenails to her little pearl earrings screamed she had no knowledge of the world, of its dangers.

She had no knowledge of the filthy things that men wanted to do to women ... that I wanted to do to her.

But she'd find out soon enough. Gracie would understand how deep my need for her went, how much I'd already claimed her as mine.

And when she did, that would be the greatest pleasure of all.

ABOUT THE AUTHOR

Want to read more by Jenika Snow? Find all her titles here:

http://jenikasnow.com/bookshelf/

Find the author at:

Newsletter: http://bit.ly/2dkihXD

www.JenikaSnow.com

Jenika_Snow@yahoo.com

Made in the USA
Las Vegas, NV
21 December 2022